W9-DEJ-406

FIGHT NIGHT

IGHT NIGHT

FIGHT NIGHT

MIRIAM TOEWS

THORNDIKE PRESS
A part of Gale, a Cengage Company

LIBRARY OF CONGRESS CIP DATA ON FILE.
CATALOGUING IN PUBLICATION FOR THIS BOOK
IS AVAILABLE FROM THE LIBRARY OF CONGRESS.

ISBN-13: 978-1-4328-9424-5 (hardcover alk. paper)

Published in 2022 by arrangement with Bloomsbury Publishing, Inc.

Printed in Mexico
Print Number: 02   Print Year: 2022

This book is dedicated to Sil and Augie
and Viv and Ty, with all my love.
And to Bob and Don, forever cool.

"An odd thing is that sadness does not necessarily become greater with age."

— John Steinbeck

■ ■ ■ ■

PART ONE:
HOME

■ ■ ■ ■

1.

DEAR DAD,

How are you? I was expelled. Have you ever heard of Choice Time? That's my favourite class. I do Choice Time at the Take-Apart Centre, which is the place in our classroom where we put on safety goggles and take things apart. It's a bit dangerous. The first half of the class we take things apart and then Madame rings a bell, which means it's the second half of the class and we're supposed to put things back together. It doesn't make sense because it takes way longer to put things back together than take them apart. I tried to talk to Mom about it, and she said I should just start putting things back together sooner, before Madame rings the bell, but when I did that Madame told me I had to wait for the bell. I told Madame about the problem with time but she didn't like my tone, which was a *lashing out* tone, which I'm supposed to be working on. Mom is in her third trimester. She's cracking up. Gord is trapped inside her. I asked her what she wanted for her birthday and she said a cold IPA and a holiday. Grandma lives with us now. She has one foot in the grave. She's not afraid of anything. I asked her where you were and she said that's the sixty-four-thousand dollar question. She said she misses Grandpa. She said that by the time she gets to heaven he'll probably have left. Men, she said. They come and they —

Today marks the beginning of our neorealist period, Grandma told me this morning. She plunked down fried potatoes on the table, and a bottle of ketchup. Fun and games! she said. She told me I have blue Nike swooshes under my eyes. She said I need to get more sleep. What's the problem, Swiv? Bad dreams?

Grandma's writing a letter to Gord, because that's the assignment I gave her and Mom at our Editorial Meeting yesterday. She gives me assignments, too. We are *co-editors*. Our family therapist was the one who told us to write letters, but Mom says we can't afford therapy anymore if all we're supposed to do is write to missing people. Grandma says she thinks it's useful. She says we can be like reporters and have our own *news desk.* She says letters start off as one thing and become another thing. But Mom mistrusts them, like photos. She hates photos. *I don't want to be frozen in a moment!*

Grandma says fragments are the only truth. Fragments of what? I asked her. Exactly! she said. She asked me what my dream was last night. I told her I dreamt that I had to write a goodbye letter using the words *one* and *blue.* Na oba! Grandma said. That'll be your assignment for today, Swivchen! She has a secret language. She didn't even ask me who the letter was for. Grandma skips over pertinent details because she's got *five minutes left to live* and doesn't want to waste it on the small picture. What if I had a dream that I was naked and locked out of my house? I asked her. Would that be my assignment? Na jungas! she said. It's happened to me many times! Grandma loves to talk about *the body.* She loves everything about the body, every nook and cranny. How can it have happened to you *many* times? I asked her. That's life! she said. You gotta love yourself, regardless. That's not *life,* I said. Being naked and locked out of your house all the time? Fun and games! she said. She was counting out her pills and laughing.

After that we had Math Class. Pencils ready! she yelled. If you've got a two thousand-piece puzzle of an Amish farm and you manage to add three pieces to the puzzle per day, how many more days will you need to stay alive to get it done? Math Class was interrupted by the doorbell. Ball Game! yelled Grandma. Who could it be? The doorbell ringer is set to "Take Me Out to the Ball Game," which Grandma forces me to sing with her during the seventh-inning stretch even if we're just watching the game in our living room. She makes me stand up for the anthem at the beginning, too. Mom doesn't stand up for the anthem because Canada is a lie and a crime scene.

It was Jay Gatsby. He wants to tear our house down. I went to the door and opened it and told him, It's yours for twenty million dollars.

He said, Listen, can I speak with your mother. You said the last time —

Twenty-five million dollars, I said.

Sorry, said Jay Gatsby, I'd like to speak with —

Thirty million dollars, capitalist, do you understand English? I slammed the door shut. Grandma said that was a bit *overkill.* He's afraid of death, said Grandma. She said it like an insult. He's lost his way! Jay Gatsby wants to tear down our house and build an underground doomsday-proof luxury vault. Jay Gatsby bought a house on a tropical island once and then forced every other person living on the island to sell their house to him so that he had the whole island to himself to do ecstasy and yoga with ex-models. He forced all the models to take pills that made their shit gold and sparkly. Mom said he's had fake muscles put into his calves. She knows this because one day she saw him on the sidewalk outside the bookstore and his calves were super skinny and three days later they were bulging and had seams on them. Mom said he went to a place in Cleveland, Ohio to get it done where you can also have your vag tightened up if you feel like it. Then you can just sit around with your *S.O.* vaping all day with your giant fake calves and stitched-up wazoo and be spied on by your *modern* thermostat which is a weapon of the state they just call "green" because of sales and Alexa and shit and practicing *mindfulness* hahahaha and just be really, really, really happy that you don't have half a fucking brain between the two of you.

15

That's how Mom talks. It's probably not true. She lies. She hates words like *modern* and *creative* and *sexuality* and she hates acronyms. She hates almost everything. Grandma told me she doesn't know how Mom was able to stop ranting long enough to get pregnant with Gord. She compared *impregnating Mom* to creeping up to the edge of an active volcano that you accidentally thought was inactive. She says Mom does the emotional work for the whole family, feeling everything ten times harder than is necessary so the rest of us can act normal. Grandma doesn't believe in privacy and thinks everything private is hilarious because she was the youngest kid to be born into a family of fifteen people. Na oba! she'll say when you're in the bathroom. Look at you sitting all by yourself in this little room with your pants around your ankles, that's *priceless*! Grandma's dad forgot what all his kids were called and accidentally gave Grandma the same name as one of the older kids. Grandma's mom used her as a *form of birth control* by putting Grandma next to her in bed for seven years. After seven years Grandma's mom *entered menopause* so she was safe, and Grandma could go sleep for the rest of her childhood in the hallway.

Remember that woman, that friend of mine, who donated her head? Grandma said yesterday. Well, she's dead. Almost every day Grandma gets a call about someone she knows being dead. This morning Grandma was watching the Blue Jays highlights and she said Vladimir Guerrero reminded her of a good friend of hers in junior high, Tina Koop. She'd just stand casually at home plate, not in a batting stance or anything, and hit a homer every time. I said Wow, what is she doing now? She's dead, said Grandma. That's how Grandma talks about her friends. She doesn't scream about it. She doesn't even cry. The only thing she and her friends talk about on the phone is dying. Grandma's friend Leona called her yesterday and said, You'll never believe this but Henry Wiebe has agreed to be cremated. What! said Grandma. That's priceless! You know why? said Leona. No, why? said Grandma. Because it's cheaper! They laughed their heads off. And more stylish! They laughed even more. Leona said Henry Wiebe was always secretly wanting to be stylish and then he found out that everyone he knew was getting cremated. When Grandma got off the phone she told me it was funny because Henry Wiebe preached to everyone for more than fifty years that cremation was a sin, but then he came into direct contact with his mortality and notorious cheapness and need to be stylish and realized that he could save money *and* be stylish by having himself cremated. But he'll be dead, I said, so how can he be stylish and save money? Grandma said, You just gotta know Henry.

You can tell when she gets phone calls about her dead friends because she pours herself an extra *schluckz* of wine to watch the Raptors and she stares at me for long stretches and quotes poetry at me even though I'm not doing anything, just sitting there watching the game with her. *Dead men naked they shall be one / With the man in the wind and the west moon.* On the days she gets the death calls she grabs at me when I walk past her and I know she wants affection, but I hate always having to be the embodiment of life. *When their bones are picked clean and the clean bones gone.* Usually I deke to the right when I pass her chair and she misses because she's really slow, but then I feel bad and I walk really slowly past her again so she can grab me. But then *she* feels bad about having tried to grab me when I don't want to be grabbed and so she *doesn't* grab me and I have to sort of just plunk down in her lap and put my arms around her. She says she's knock, knock, knockin' on heaven's door and she is *at 110 percent peace with that.* She says when she kicks the bucket I should just put her in a pickle jar and go outside and play already.

Our next class was How to Dig a Winter Grave. Grandma said when she was a small kid she went to a funeral in North Dakota and discovered that all the people who died in the winter there had to wait around until the spring to be buried. I was horrified! said Grandma. She heckled the undertaker. They didn't know how to dig a winter grave?! Here's what you do, she said. Heat up coals and lay them on the ground until it melts. Dig up that layer of dirt. Reheat the coals and lay them down on the ground again until another layer of dirt melts. Dig it up. Keep doing that until you've got a six-foot hole. Done! You don't wait until the spring to bury people. What nonsense! Let's phone North Dakota to see if they're still making people wait until the spring to be buried, I said. Let's do it, said Grandma. I called the North Dakota Board of Funerals. The man said, Yes, that's just how it is here. Delayed burials are a *necessary evil* in North Dakota.

Grandma likes to sit on the top step of our front porch and water the flowers and fall asleep in the sun. She tilts her head way back to feel the warm sun on her face. The instant she falls asleep she loses her grip on the hose and it flips all over the place and sprays her awake and then she knows she's had her nap and also accomplished a *household task.* She sprays cops when they have their windows down and are cruising slowly past our house because she hates them after what they did when Grandpa died, and just period. When they get out of the car and walk up to her she says things like, Here comes Rocket Man! Send in the clowns! The cops smile because they think she's just a crazy old lady. But she really means business. She hates them. She doesn't *want* to hate anybody but she can't help it and she isn't even going to pray about it because she thinks God secretly hates them too. When they ask all the usual questions, she doesn't say a word. She points the hose at their *little armoured feet* if even one inch of a boot is on our yard and forces them to back onto the sidewalk.

Grandma likes to tell Mom we've accomplished household tasks every day because Mom is having a complete nervous breakdown and a geriatric pregnancy which doesn't mean she's going to push an old geezer out of her vag, it means she's too old to be up the stump and is *so exhausted* and when she comes home from rehearsals she's all, God, what a mess, god you guys, what a dump, you can't pour fat down the drain, these pipes are ancient, you can't overload the toilet with toilet paper, why are there conchigliettes everywhere, can't you two pick up a dish or put this shit away or have you ever even heard of *household tasks?* Mom's latest *domestic* freak-out is that she always has to put all the food that's in the fridge at the very outer edges of the racks so that it's entirely visible to Grandma, otherwise Grandma thinks there's no food because she can't see it, and she doesn't move things around to see the food in the back of the fridge and then she orders take-out or just eats ice cream or bacon or hand-fuls of cereal from the box. So now Mom lines everything up in a row on the outer edges of the fridge racks with labels like THIS IS LENTIL CHILI! EAT IT! THIS IS KALE SALAD! EAT IT! Grandma doesn't eat anything green. Not a single thing, ever. It's like Samson and his hair. He can't cut it or he'll lose his strength. Grandma can't eat green things. She can detect green things in her food when Mom tries to hide them in there. *I'm not going to spend my last five minutes on earth eating rabbit food!* She takes a long time, like it's an opera or something, after she's detected the green things, to slowly pick them out of her food one by one and put them on the table beside her plate. Mom sighs and takes the pile and eats it herself but she never stops trying to trick Grandma and Grandma never stops not being tricked. Grandma won't eat red soup. Mom made borscht for us and Grandma said I am *not* eating red soup. Why not? Because I don't *eat* red soup!

Mom says to me, Don't say up the stump, don't say that thing about a skunk's asshole, don't say vag, don't say shit tickets. And Mom says to Grandma, Use the subtitles *or* top volume when you watch *Call the Midwife,* not both. Why would you use both! What difference does it make to you if I use both? It's using too many of your senses at once! Na oba! It's up to me how I use my senses! Grandma loses her hearing aids in the exact same places every day. I try to keep all her dead batteries in an old thyme tin to bring them to the right part of the garbage dump but yesterday Mom was *so exhausted* from her rehearsals and carrying Gord around 24-7 that she mistakenly shook the batteries into the spaghetti sauce and we had to pick them out at dinnertime and make tiny piles of them next to our plates, which in Mom's case is next to piles of Kleenex from blowing her nose constantly.

At dinner Mom said she doesn't know why she's so tired all the time, the third trimester is supposed to be one of *renewed energy*. She doesn't even have the energy to play Dutch Blitz. She said she's supposed to have a burst of energy to clean and organize the house in preparation for Gord's arrival. The burst is called the *nesting instinct*. I have it! I said. I'm the one who cleans everything! Mom rubbed my hair around and said, Oh, that's so cute, you've got the nesting instinct. Which is obviously not cute. I don't want to have *instincts*. I said Grandma, listen to this. First try, mister. Second try, mister, third try, mister, and . . . you're out! Grandma didn't hear me. She pretended to. Don't try me, mister? she said. I shouted it again. Na kjint! said Grandma. She was still pretending. I shouted as loud as I could, and Mom said Swiv! Jesus fucking Christ!

There is the sound of continuous screaming coming out of Grandma's bedroom from women having babies or from the babies themselves being forced to be born or from people being murdered or from people discovering the bodies of the murdered people. Grandma says British women sure scream a lot when they discover dead bodies. I would too, I told her. No, no, she said. It's a *body*. It's nuscht! Grandma rides her Gazelle for fifteen minutes while she's watching her shows. She says hoooooo in between strides and afterwards, Goot, goot, goot. Gownz yenook. Only her dying and dead friends know her secret language. She takes lines from her shows and practices them on me all day with a British accent. Swiv, darling, we must make a dash for the continent!

Grandma said in Editorial Meeting that I should say "plug your piehole" silently to myself, if I have to, so I don't get Mom riled up because Mom is *city* now and with Gord and everything. Grandma says that when Mom goes scorched earth our only hope for survival is to take cover in a different room and wait for it to blow over. For Pythia to stop ranting at Delphi. Grandma says I should try to turn Mom's *oracling* into elegant hexameters like the Greeks did. She said a hexameter is a poem with a curse built into it.

Grandma has known Mom since Mom was born on the *hottest day in history* before the invention of fans and AC. The room was

a furnace! said Grandma. *Blood and fire!*
She said when Mom was born the doctor
was so useless at removing babies from
women that Grandma had to say to him
would you please get your hands out of me
and let me do this myself. Mom finally
popped out angry and crimson-red, like a
tiny Satan. When Mom goes scorched earth
she swishes oregano oil around in her
mouth to prevent her from saying horrible
things she'll regret and to boost her im-
munity even though there's no scientific
evidence that it does. Grandma told Mom
today, before Mom went to rehearsal, that I
hold it in when I'm doing the Sudoku in
the morning and then I miss the boat. Mom
said, What are you talking about, boat, and
Grandma told her I have a fixation about
finishing the Sudoku before I do anything,
including Editorial Meeting and having a
bowel movement, and then my *stool* retreats
back inside me and colours my outlook for
the whole day and is probably the thing that
causes the Nike swooshes under my eyes.
Swiv is sponsored by Nike? said Mom. Slay
me. Mom stared hard at me like she was
trying to see right through my skin to the
piles and piles of built-up stool inside me.
Then she said, Hmmm, just keep trying,
Swiv. Just try to relax, sweetheart. She slid

her thumbs along my Nike swooshes. She hugged me and then she left.

I don't know why saying *bowel movement* and *stool* is better than vag and piehole. It doesn't matter what words you use in life, it's not gonna prevent you from suffering.

Two weeks ago Grandma gave her Winnipeg Jets sweatpants to a guy who came to the door and today when Mom and I were walking home from therapy we saw that guy sitting on the curb outside the 7-Eleven wearing them and singing "Just a Closer Walk with Thee." Then we looked even closer and we saw that Grandma was sitting on the curb too and also singing "Just a Closer Walk with Thee." Grandma wasn't wearing her track suit or cargoes, she was wearing a short skirt and sitting with her legs apart because it was hard for her to sit on a curb and I could see her underwear, which gave me my nervous tic of coughing. Grandma loves to be naked. She proudly tells the same story to every new person about how she inadvertently did a strip tease for a guy in Mexico City and he really, *really* enjoyed it. Grandma and Mom argue about Grandma giving things away, but Grandma says after the doctors killed almost everyone she loved she had to ask herself how she would survive grief and her answer was Who can I help? Grandma says doctors killed her family. Doctors killed my husband. Doctors killed my sister. Doctors killed my daughter. When she says that, Mom quietly tells me not to say anything except yeah, it's true. Or, I agree with you, Grandma. You're right. If Mom or I say anything else, like how can that be or that's an exaggeration or anything like that, Grandma will erupt and probably have a heart attack because she already has so much obsolete hardware in her chest and a long scar that runs down almost her entire torso like a zipper. Grandma says doctors killed everyone when she's mad or when she's drinking Mom's special rum from Italy, which is just ordinary Canadian rum that Mom poured into a special Italian bottle. Sometimes Grandma cries. She feels guilty. Then Mom has to sit down and hold Grandma's hands and run through every scenario with her to make her see that she's not. Grandma only loves Dr. De Sica. He's young and handsome and Italian. He's keeping her alive. He checks in on her. When the phone rings Grandma says oh, is that my De Sica? When she goes to his office she acts tough. She lies. So De Sica has to guess what's wrong with her.

When I help Grandma get undressed for her shower I run my finger down her scar and go zzzzzzzip! Step out of your skin, ma'am! She sits on a plastic shower chair that Mom found in someone's garbage — when Mom brought it home Grandma said ha ha, obviously *someone* around here bought the farm — laughing and laughing and I lather her up with lavender French soap her friend William gave her for helping him fight his landlord and write a letter to his arrogant brother. I have to lift up her rolls of fat to get in the creases and even wash her giant butt and boobs and the bottoms of her hard, crispy feet and her toes which twist around each other. Then I have to soak up the three inches of water on the bathroom floor so she doesn't slip and fall because that would be the end, my friend, she says. Then I dry her off and brush her soft white baby hair and put the bobby pins back in to pull it away from her face because Mom gave her a ridiculous fashionable haircut called a Wispy Silver Bob that goes in her eyes, and put her hearing aids back into her ears which I hate doing because you really have to push them in there hard and I think I'm hurting her even though she says I'm not. And I have to help her get dressed in clean cotton underwear — I always have to tell her to put her hand on my back for balance so she doesn't tip over when I'm scrunched around her feet trying to get them to go into the holes of her panties — and her track suit or her cargo pants which she likes because they can carry all her painkillers and her nitro spray and her whodunnit, which this week is called *FOE,* and extra hearing aid batteries around with her. Then I find her red felt slippers and her glasses which I clean with my breath and the bottom of my t-shirt and put a fresh nitro patch on her arm which blasts dynamite into her veins and I hold her hand all the way to her bed taking slow, slow steps because she's dizzy from the heat of the shower and the exertion of laughing so hard.

When she starts snoring I sometimes smoke a Marlie from Mom's pack that she stores in the top drawer of her dresser for the *goddamn glorious day* she's not pregnant with Gord and not *so exhausted.* I go out on the back deck and take just a couple of puffs and I look at the sky. Or I throw clothespins into a pail and try not to miss. If I miss, you're not coming back. If I get them all in, you're coming back. I started with the pail in my lap so it was really easy not to miss but then it seemed *too* easy a way to make you come back and then you didn't come back anyway, so now I keep moving the pail further and further away.

Grandma is supposed to sleep with this machine on her face that has a tube and a box filled with water so she doesn't stop breathing, but she hates it. Grandma doesn't move when she's sleeping but Mom flings her arms and legs around and talks and yells in her sleep. Grandma says Mom has a tiny bit of PTSD still, plus she's searching. I asked Grandma what Mom's searching for and she said, Oh, you name it. PTSD and searching don't end when we're asleep. Mom and Grandma know things about each other that they just have to *contend with* because that's how it is. They don't mind. They know each other. I found a letter that Mom wrote you six hundred years ago about the way she likes to sleep but obviously you never got it or maybe you got it but left it behind because you're travelling light.

In case you want to know about how Mom likes to sleep I'll copy it out for you. (Mom doesn't know how to spell so I fixed the mistakes.)

I don't want to talk about this or argue about this cuz time is too short, but there were a bunch of things leading up to this . . . First of all you were so annoyed that I was up so late texting. I was texting with Carol about the very exciting news of Frankie's new baby! The details. That's Lidia's granddaughter! Then you pretended that you weren't annoyed but I could tell you still were cuz you yanked things around on the bed angrily. You said that I was rejecting your "tender" gesture of making the bed into something I hate. You making the bed was not tender! You know I don't like to sleep stuck rigidly in an envelope unable to move around and the air pockets make me cold! Is it tender to force a person to sleep the way you want to sleep even when she hates it like that? Is that "tender"??? No, it's not. You know it's not. Then you stomp upstairs to sulk and sleep alone in your freezing cold envelope. Okay, hope you're over it. I'm gonna sleep the way I want to sleep. It's really not too much to ask to have my blanket and sheet a certain way. Have yours tucked in who the fuck cares! xox

Even when Grandma is fast asleep and snoring, if I put one finger gently on her shoulder she'll burst to life and stretch her arms out to me and smile and say, Sweetheartchen! I ask her every time, Did you detect my presence? But she never hears me because she takes her hearing aids out to sleep and she just laughs and holds on to my wrists like they're reins on a horse. She can't believe she keeps waking up alive and is really amazed and grateful about it which is what all the pamphlets at therapy say we're supposed to be feeling about every new day.

Naturally there's a fucking conchigliette in my shoe! Those were the last words of Mom this morning before she slammed the door on her way to rehearsal. Grandma said, That's a family classic, Swiv, write that down. Then Grandma shouted, Good luck! Have fun! Don't work too hard! She says that every single time a person leaves. She says that where she's from it's the most *subversive* thing you can say because they didn't believe in luck and fun was a sin and work was the *only* thing you were supposed to do. Almost every day Mom finds a conchigliette in her shoe or stuck to her script or somewhere else. It's Grandma's favourite food but when her arthritis is bad it's hard for her to open the box and then when she finally gets it open the conchigliettes fly everywhere and I sweep them up but not very well because Mom always finds them in her stuff. The conchigliettes go into *every-*

body's stuff but Mom is the one who freaks out about it. Grandma loves them because they're small and if she's having one of her trigeminal neuralgia days she doesn't even have to chew them, they just slither down her throat. Grandma is trying to find someone who will drill a hole in her head because she's heard that's the most effective way of getting rid of trigeminal neuralgia, which is nicknamed the suicide disease because it's the most painful physical experience a human being can have and you just want to kill yourself. But nobody wants to drill a hole into Grandma's head because of her age. They stop drilling holes into people at around age sixty. Remember that, Swiv! Grandma said.

After Mom left, Grandma asked me to write a list of her medications. Not in cursive, she said, print it out. None of those young ambulance drivers can read cursive, they think it's Arabic, they're just tap tap tap all day on their cameras. She means phones. I can't read your old cursive either, I told her. She read the medications out loud to me so I could print them out.

Amlodipine 7.5 mg OD
Lisinopril 10 mg OD
Furosemide 20 mg OD

Pravastatin 20 mg OD
Colchicine .6 mg OD
Omeprazole 20 mg OD
Metoprolol 50 mg b.i.d.
Oxcarbazepine 300 mg OD

It's funny that it says "OD" after every drug, I said.

That's my back-up plan, she said. Just pulling your leg. She said it means One a Day.

What's b.i.d.?

Bis in Die, she said. It's Latin for twice a day. Grandma used to be a nurse. She got hazed by the older nurses in her first week of being a nurse. They threw her into a stainless steel tub and poured ether all over her until she began to pass out and freeze to death. She begged them to stop. She thinks this is one of the funniest things that's ever happened to her. She organizes her pills into little groups, one of each, and puts them into the days of the week in her plastic pill box. Grandma says she has to keep doing this and not ever get so confused that she has to go to the bubble pack system, which costs money, so forget it. When she drops pills on the floor accidentally, if she *notices* she drops them, she says, Bombs away, Swiv! When I hear her say that, I come running and drop down onto the floor and scramble around by her feet picking them up and also picking up hearing aid batteries and conchigliettes and pieces from her Amish farm puzzle.

Today Grandma finally remembered I was supposed to be in school even though I'd already been home for fifty-nine days. Why aren't you in school? she asked. I didn't say anything because she sounded like a cop and she never answers their questions so why should I. Fighting? said Grandma. I didn't move. Then I did what Grandma does when the cops come, which is she holds up an imaginary cellphone like she's recording them. She said she already knew it must be about fighting because I kept coming home with dried blood on my face and bruises on my neck and tufts of hair ripped out of my head and my jacket missing an arm. Then we were quiet for a long, long time, just sitting there making small noises, not words. I put my fake phone on the table with a big swooping gesture like I was doing her a favour by not recording her anymore. I smashed breadcrumbs on the tablecloth with my thumb. Grandma shook her pill case a few times and lined up her mouse and pad and laptop in a straight row. I watched her fingers moving around on the table. Her nails needed clipping again. I couldn't remember where I'd left the nail clipper. I looked at her face. She was smiling.

I'm glad you're here with me, she said.

Madame said I had one too many fights, which if I knew the exact number of fights I was *supposed* to have then there wouldn't be this bullshit, I said.

Hmmmmmmmm, said Grandma.

They said we're communists which is why dad is being tortured somewhere.

He's not being tortured anywhere, said Grandma. Who said that?

The kids I fought, I said. How do you know he's not being tortured? I picked up my cellphone again and aimed it at her.

Grandma asked me if I wanted to continue our Editorial Meeting but I didn't answer. Then she asked me if I knew what bioluminescence was. I smashed breadcrumbs with my thumb and kept my piehole shut. It's one's ability to create light from within, said Grandma. Like a firefly. I think you have that, Swivchen. You have a fire inside you and your job is to not let it go out. I'm too young to have a job, I said. There are fish that have it too, said Grandma. Ostracods. I clamped my mouth shut and folded my arms. First try, mister, she said. Okay, second try, mister: let's go onto the roof instead. She said she wanted to go onto the flat part of our roof, the roof that's over the kitchen and dining room upstairs and spell out the words REBEL STRONGHOLD with rocks or whatever we could find that wouldn't blow away. She said Jay Gatsby will be able to see it. I had to go behind Grandma and push her up the stairs and remind her to keep breathing. She stopped on every stair and turned around to look at me and made big exaggerated breathing sounds to prove to me she was still alive. We don't have rocks, I said. When we made it to the roof she said, How about we use those clothespins lying all over the back yard? I need them for other stuff, I said. Plus it would take a million of them. How about we use books instead?

That was not a good idea, holy shit.

Mom came home from rehearsal and noticed that her books from the special shelf on the third floor — which are supposed to be *tight, no breathing room, and perfectly upright* — were not on the shelf at all and she went into full-on scorched earth. What the holy hell! she yelled from up there. I hadn't expected her to go to the third floor at all because of Gord and her exhaustion but she'd heard some beeping coming from a smoke detector and said for fuck's sake, guess this is on me, because she knows I can't reach it even if I stand on a chair, and then went stomping up there with a new battery. Now she was yelling that if I had pawned books from the special shelf she'd fucking lose her mind! Which I wanted to tell her was too late. She said this because one time I had pawned six of her reject books — not ones that came from her special shelf, but ones that were already in a fucking box to go to the diabetes foundation — so I could buy one goddamn Archie Digest which she disapproved of because of female stereotypes and would never give me money for! I yelled back from the bottom of the stairs. She yelled from upstairs, Those are books that help me to live! Those books are my life!

Get down here! I yelled back. I'm your goddamn life!

When she came downstairs I held out her oregano oil. Take it, take it, I said, so she could calm down but she threw it at the living room wall and the bottle broke and oil trickled down over that Diego Rivera print I got her in Detroit for her birthday with money from Grandma. Then she started to cry and told me she was so sorry, so sorry. I hugged her and said it was okay because the dripping oil added character to the print which is what she always says about things that get damaged. Like if I scrape an entire layer of skin off my face from falling on the ice in King of the Castle, which I am the champion of, she tells me having one less layer of skin adds character, and also her books weren't gone, they were just out on the roof.

When Mom climbed the stairs and looked at the words on the roof spelled with her books, she put her hand on her mouth. She told me quietly from behind her hand that she would be downstairs and that I could gather up all of the books and put them back alphabetically on her special shelf, tight and perfectly upright. She was so eerily quiet. I wondered if Gord was afraid inside her. Right then I wanted to tell her that it was Grandma's idea to spell out words on the roof but you don't rat on a comrade. It was dark by the time I got all the books back into the house and alphabetical and tight and upright on her shelf. I went downstairs and Mom was making dinner and laughing with Grandma. I don't understand adults. I hate them. I don't know if Grandma took responsibility for her actions and confessed to Mom. Probably not. Grandma was the one who got me kicked out of school in the first place because she was the one who told me that people sometimes have to be punched in the face to get the message to leave you alone and not bully you, but only after double-digit times of trying to use words to no avail and only up to the age of ten or eleven. Don't tell Mom I said any of that, she said. Because she's a Quaker now or something. But you have to defend yourself.

After dinner, me and Grandma helped Mom with her lines which made Mom laugh so hard she peed a small amount, a teaspoonful. Grandma drank two glasses of William's homemade plonk. I was nervous that it would make her start talking about the doctors killing everyone but it just made her dramatic. When she read Jack's lines she stood up from the table while Mom was laughing her head off to say: "I kiss you, but it's as though my kisses hurtle off a cliff. You take off your clothes, but you're not naked. What can we do, then? What will happen?"

Then Grandma said, Oh that reminds me, that reminds me! She had another story of epic nudity. One Christmas centuries ago Grandma was young and *squatting* on the sixth floor of an auto parts warehouse in West Berlin that was right beside the Wall.

You know *the Wall,* Swiv, the *Wall!* (No, I don't.) And she looked out the window into East Berlin and saw a young German soldier all by himself marching around with this giant coat that was too big for him and his giant rifle dangling awkwardly off his little shoulder. Grandma watched him for a while until she could get his attention and then she waved and he waved back and smiled and stopped marching. Grandma breathed on the glass and wrote *Fröhilche Weih-nachten* in the steam backwards for the soldier to read and then the soldier hastily spelled out a message of his own to Grandma in the snow which was *Ich bin ein Gefangener des Staates* and then she slowly took off all her clothes while he stood there by himself in the *dusky square* with light snow falling and all his heavy artillery and coat and little shoulders. When she was totally naked she curtsied, and then the soldier blew her kisses and clapped and they waved goodbye. Mom said, Oh my god, that is INSANE! I thought so too but not in the way the two of them thought it was but in the way you go to a locked-up hospital with guards. Well, I was young, said Grandma. I'm young and I don't do that, I said. Not yet, said Grandma. It's a memory now. I wonder if the soldier remembers that night.

Mom got up and hugged Grandma. I'm sure he does, she said.

2.

This morning the curtain to Mom's bedroom, which is really a living room, which is why there isn't a normal door, was torn off the curtain rod. The curtain rod was torn off the wall, the remote control was smashed and the battery was gone, the hairbrush handle was broken from being thrown at the cutlery thing in the kitchen, the cutlery thing in the kitchen was chipped from having the hairbrush thrown at it and the necklace that you gave her with our initials on it was ripped into a million pieces which in addition to hearing aid batteries, Grandma's pills, Amish farm puzzle pieces and conchigliettes I now have to crawl around and pick up. It's a good thing I can't go to school anymore so I have all day for picking up everybody's shit.

Before Mom went to rehearsal she grabbed me and pinned my head to her rib cage. I couldn't escape. She said I'm sorry!

I'm sorry! It was about her rampage. I made a joke but she wanted me to take it all seriously. It was too disturbing to take seriously. You're up the stump, Mom, I said, you're on an *emotional rollercoaster!* Were you talking to dad? I asked. Something like that, she said. Something like dad or something like talking, I said. She said, Something like all of that.

Mom told me and Grandma that she was going to a Russian spa and teahouse with someone in the cast after rehearsal today where she would be whipped with branches to get her blood flowing. Jack? I said. No, not *Jack,* she said. Jack is a *character,* Swiv! Be careful, Gord, I said silently. Mom said she wouldn't sit in the hot tub because of Gord. Grandma said it was funny that a hundred years ago we — which doesn't mean *we* — had narrowly escaped getting whipped and murdered by Russians and now Mom was voluntarily paying big bucks to get whipped and murdered by Russians. But she gets tea afterwards, I said. Mom said she'd prefer hot vodka although not this time because of Gord, who gets blamed for preventing Mom from doing every fun thing in life. Don't smoke! I yelled at her. Then Mom opened the door and said what the hell is this? Grandma and I yelled *RAIN*

44

at the same time. Mom stomped around looking for an umbrella that wasn't *broke to shit* and Grandma called out, Bye! See you in the funny papers!

Today Grandma is feeling dizzy when she bends over. So don't bend over! I said. She said she finally had an excellent bowel movement. It's been six days. It's not a record. What's your record, Grandma? Ecuador in '74 was a record. She asked me if I'd heard anything about *the divine feminine.* She said she should bring her crossword puzzle into the washroom with her more often. She couldn't find her glasses or her address book. I held them up to her face. They were on the table in front of her. Well, of all things! I'm not with it today!

Then Grandma got talking for about one and a half hours, which took up all of Editorial Meeting, about her old life in that town of escaped Russians. She can't believe she lived there for sixty-two years except for the few months she squatted in Berlin accidentally when she went to Germany to visit her older sister who was living in *the Black Forest,* which is the home of the cuckoo clock, she said. Mom should go there, I said. To the Black Forest? said Grandma. To the home of the cuckoo clock, I said. It makes me shudder! said Grandma.

I was a *maverick*! She was talking about her town. It worked against us, she said. When she was a kid her father protected her from Willit Braun Senior, the uber-schultz of the village who was a *classic tyrant,* pompous, authoritarian, insecure, frustrated, self-pitying, resentful, envious, vain and vindictive, and with a mighty chip on his shoulder and dumb. Also, he embodied the fascist notion of a superior group, which he thought was us. Well, not all of us. The men among us. What a wingnut. You can write those things down, Swiv, she said. Just make a little note of that.

Well, I'm recording it, I told her. I held up my phone and she shook her head. Oh right, I always forget about your camera. Make sure it has juice. Was it a cult? I said. No, said Grandma. Well, yes, possibly. It was!

Grandma divides the people from her town into MB or EMC. She is EMC. She says the MBs think they're the only ones going to heaven. They were also the first ones in town to sing in four-part harmony. For the EMCs that was a mortal sin until Sid Reimer's dad brought it in to the church. And he brought a pump organ which was also a sin. He was very instrumental in moving the church forward.

When Grandma grew up, she protected

herself from Willit Braun. And she protected Mom from him too, and everyone in her family, even Grandpa, who really liked that about her. *He was all for it!* He couldn't fight for himself. He couldn't do it. He would get very quiet and go for long, long walks. Very long walks. Sometimes until his feet bled. Talking about fighting and escaping reminded her of a friend of hers from that town who she and their other friend helped to escape from her violent husband. The woman's daughter and her friends got together and hatched a plan to whisk her away to Montreal where the daughter lived in a *loft* apartment. But the friend felt so guilty she returned to the town and to her husband six months later. Then all the women prayed that he would die. What else could they do? And he did, eventually. It took five years. This can be today's math class, said Grandma. If it takes five years to kill a guy with prayer, and it takes six people a day to pray, then how many prayers of pissed off women praying every day for five years does it take to pray a guy to death?

Grandma sorted her meds on the table with the edge of her credit card while she waited for my answer. Ten thousand, nine hundred and fifty prayers, I said. Whoa, she said. Am I right? I asked. Who knows, she said, I believe you!

After that I went with Grandma on the streetcar to meet her friends at the Duke of York. I went because she was dizzy and had to lean on me. Every six months the group of them get together to celebrate that they're still living. Grandma wore her red slippers instead of shoes because her right foot was *puffed up like a blowfish.* That's the leg they took the vein out of to put into her chest. Look at the way my track pants cover them up, she said. Nobody will notice I'm wearing slippers. Before we left I spent twenty-five minutes helping her get her compression socks on. She almost went with one compression sock only because she was impatient but I forced her to let me put the other one on because it looked stupid with just one. Halfway to The Duke of York her diuretic *kicked in* and we had to make an emergency stop to find a bathroom. We got off the streetcar and went into the first building we saw which was the corporate headquarters of OBTRON. It had a lot of glass and shiny black furniture including the desk where the security guy was sitting. He didn't look at us the whole time. He had a gun. He stared at all his TVs and said, I'm asking you to leave right now.

Surely there's a washroom in this building

that I could use, said Grandma.

I'm afraid not, he said, they're not designated for public use.

She really has to go! I told him.

You don't have to yell at me, miss, I can hear you. I told you they're not designated for public use.

Her diuretic kicked in on the streetcar and she'll spring a leak if you don't let her use the fucking washroom, you fascist prick! I said.

Swiv, said Grandma. She pretended to slice her throat with her finger. The guy finally looked at us and got up and came around to the front of the desk with his hand on his gun. Grandma asked him if it was all right with him if she peed in one of those giant planters by the window. He said no, he couldn't authorize her to do that. Do it! I told Grandma. I'm authorizing it! She said no, no, we'll find a place. She told the security guy she was very tempted to let 'er rip right there in the lobby on that shiny floor and he said ma'am, you do not have a constitutional right to use fighting words with me. Then Grandma started talking about constitutional rights but she was huffing and puffing and also dizzy still, and sort of teetering around and it was hard for her to talk. You're gonna have a goddamn cardiac event, Grandma, I told her. I'm telling De Sica. De Sica! said Grandma. Did he call? Don't let this be the hill you die on! I said. Hooooooooo, said Grandma. You're right. What a ridiculous last stand. I took Grandma's hand and we went to the Tim Hortons next door and bought two Boston cream doughnuts so they would give us the code to the washroom.

Grandma said that I have a slight, slight, slight, *slight* tendency at times to go a bit overboard. You were the one who said we have to defend the most vulnerable amongst us, I told her, and that's you! I pointed at her slippers and compression socks. You said in every sport defence is job one! Then she told me that the security guard was not the main culprit. It was the rich owners of the company he worked for. He was just doing his job the way he'd been told to do his job by not letting ladies pee wherever they wanted to in the building. Grandma said he could have broken the rules and let her use the washroom but he was too afraid of it all getting caught on tape and then losing his job and then his family starving. She said *he* was the most vulnerable. Then I was mad because I had only been trying to do the right thing. I walked too fast for Grandma so she couldn't breathe. Then I felt like crying because I was mad at myself and everyone. I slowed down so Grandma wouldn't die. She was busy trying to survive and didn't notice that there were tears in my eyes. Fighting is so hard and yet we're never supposed to stop!

I lay down and tried to have a nap in the booth at the Duke of York while Grandma and her friends had lunch and talked about their bodies. Wilda has blue finger syndrome and her pelvic floor has dropped. And about doctors killing everyone. And about misunderstandings and *Call the Midwife* and capitalism and *espionage* and existential angst and the royal family and Iran and bus tours versus cruises and grandchildren and cotton versus silk underwear and living wills, and even you. Do you know where he is? Wilda asked Grandma. I had my eyes closed and waited to hear the answer. Then Wilda said ah, right. Grandma must have pointed at me and shook her head, zipped her lips and thrown away the key. One of the women, Ida, asked the others if they were going the *assisted dying route.* She told the women that her friend in Ajax had gone the assisted dying route and her last words were ahhhh, peace. Wilda said piece of what? She was joking. One last slice of cherry cheese cake? They all laughed and then they all sighed. Grandma said oh, but isn't that beautiful. She means it but I can tell from her voice that it also makes her sad and mad that Grandpa and Auntie Momo couldn't go the assisted dying route. Will you go that route, Elvira? Wilda asked. Assisted dying? said Grandma. Of course she would! She had filled out all the forms the other day at Raptors halftime. It's very straightforward, she said. Wilda said she was worried about saying goodbye to everyone before she died. How would she get around to it all when she'd be so busy with dying. Grandma said no problem. Let's say goodbye now and get it over with! We're friends, we love each other, we know it, we've had good times, and one day we'll be dead, whether we're assisted or not. So, goodbye! They all thought that was a good idea so they all said goodbye to each other then and got it over with. Then Grandma told them the whole story of her diuretic kicking in and the guy with the gun and they laughed and laughed. He just didn't understand! one of them said. They just don't understand. *They just don't understand.* When the bill came they all had to stare at it and think for half an hour and then they all put the wrong amount of money in the centre of the table and Wilda had to count it over five times and yell at everyone to stop interrupting her.

On the streetcar home I counted twelve people from *all walks of life* who looked at Grandma's slippers. She didn't care. She laughed. I wanted her to pull her track pants further over them but she was sitting down so her track pants rode up instead, even revealing her compression socks and parts of her legs. She also farted on the streetcar and in between *gales of laughter* when she could barely breathe she whispered to me that she was really sorry for embarrassing me and that when I was a baby and we were in public places together she would say that I was the one who had farted, not her. I'll have to teach Gord to be strong and alert. Babies are fall guys. Then Grandma fell asleep with her head on my shoulder for six stops.

Two people standing in the aisle started arguing. The lady said to the man, Listen, you have to understand your gross factor for any woman under the age of forty. The man said: You could say under thirty-five. No, really, dude, said the woman, forty. The man said she was crazy. He said she should say thirty-five. She said she wouldn't say thirty-five, no way. They stared out the window in opposite directions.

We stopped at the Sev to get microwave popcorn for the Raptors game. The same guy was there sitting on the curb wearing Grandma's Winnipeg Jets sweatpants. He didn't recognize her. He asked me for change.

I have none, I said.

Robert, he said.

Sorry, I have none.

Robert.

Sorry, I have none, Robert.

Mom came home late after rehearsal and said there were cop cars on either end of our street. What did you guys do now? she asked us.

The doorbell rang. Ball Game! It was Jay Gatsby. He had seen Mom coming home. She opened the door and said fifteen million dollars. Jay Gatsby said please, can we just —

Mom said thirty million dollars cash. She slammed the door.

The doorbell rang again. Ball Game! It was the two cops from the two ends of the street. They were all smiles. They had their hands on their guns. They asked Mom if they could ask her a few questions. She said no. They asked Mom if she had seen any suspicious activity around here lately. Yours, she said. Close the door, honey, said Grandma. Mom asked the cop if she could see his gun for a sec. Honey! said Grandma. She hobbled over to the front door and said out, out, thank you, Knight Rider, and then closed it.

I made conchigliettes with cheese. We ate it watching the game. Grandma drank red wine and Mom drank water because of Buzzkill. Don't call Gord that, I said. Mom said she was kidding, but that was a lie. I just love it when Kyle Lowry gets mad, said Grandma. Mom was silent. I don't know why McCaw always does those flybys in the corners, said Grandma. Does he think he's performing *The Nutcracker*? It doesn't seem as effective a defence as when they just stand their ground. I mean get your arms up, plant your feet, right Swiv? I nodded. All they have to do is wait a second for Mc-Caw to do his leaping and then they make their threes, said Grandma. Ridiculous! Mom didn't say anything. Tears were on her face.

Grandma got up and sat down beside Mom and patted her leg and asked her how her day had gone. She put Mom's feet into her lap and rubbed them. Mom said she thinks she offended her stage manager. Her stage manager had told Mom that she had no time to read books and Mom said to the stage manager you have time to watch Netflix for three hours every evening but no time to read books? After that Mom said the stage manager was just being *weird.* She didn't give Mom notes on time so Mom missed a bunch of cues and looked like an idiot. I think you're just paranoid, Mom, I said. Because of Gord and everything. Mom said pregnancy doesn't make you paranoid. I'd be paranoid if I had a whole other completely separate person growing inside of me, I said. Well, make sure you use birth control then, she said. She has to say disgusting things. She said she'd send the stage manager a text apologizing. After that she stopped crying. She took just one sip of Grandma's wine. Then she said Serge Ibaka is *inordinately* handsome. She said *oh fuck off with your happiness* during the Keg commercials and threw popcorn at the TV which I picked up and threw into the air and caught in my mouth every time. Then she started getting worried again because the stage manager wasn't texting back to say it was okay. Grandma said don't worry, honey, she's probably just busy watching her Netflix.

3.

Last night I slept with Mom. Gord was tucked right in between us. Mom slept with her hand on her chin like she was thinking all night long.

On her way to rehearsal this morning Mom told me not to forget to let the rat guy in.

Grandma is watching her shows on rotation. She watches the same episodes of *Call the Midwife* and *Midsomer Murders* and *Miss Fisher* two or three times because she always falls asleep during them, even with all the screaming and killing, and she thinks it's unlikely that she would fall asleep at the same place in the show twice so every time she watches she's picking up new clues and information. Poor Grandma. Today she has the Triple Scoop Sundae. Gout, trigeminal neuralgia, angina. With a topping of arthritis. I was clipping her toenails and trying to straighten out her toes. Her tree roots, she calls them. Ho! she said. Are you kidding me? It's only pain. We don't worry about pain. It's not life-threatening. It is not those who can inflict the most but those who can suffer the most who will conquer, she said. If you say so, I said. That's an Irish guy, a soldier of the republic who said that, she told me. Do you know *his* name? I asked. Is it Cipher? Terence MacSwiney, she said. Have you heard of the 1916 Easter Rising? Obviously not, I said. You mean Jesus? I was serious. She began to laugh but it turned into a cough. I had to stop clipping and she had to use her nitro spray three times which is the maximum number of times before you call 911 or basically die.

Ball Game! It was the rat guy. He said Mom had called him because she'd seen a rat. Grandma said *she* was the one who'd seen a rat. This big, she said. She held out her hands. Long tail. Black. It ran out of the *foyer* and then behind the piano and then went flying over there behind the *china cabinet* and then around into the kitchen and down the basement stairs. Hmmm, said the rat guy. It wasn't a mouse? Grandma said it was definitely not a mouse. She shuffled back to her bedroom with her walker and left me alone with the rat guy. He looked all over the house and said he didn't see any rat signs. He threw some rat poison in the crawlspace in the basement. He wanted to show me what he was doing but I didn't want to get anywhere near that crawlspace and I stayed upstairs. Then he sat down at the dining room table with me and started filling out his report and invoice. He spoke very quietly. He said animals, even rats, are just trying to take care of their babies and survive. He said divorce just breaks you down and then you have to re-invent yourself. I nodded. He said he communes with every animal. When he went to Mexico with his wife, pelicans landed on his head. Dogs protect him in strange houses when he's fighting pests. Seagulls follow him around. He searches for inner peace and balance. He told me I had to get in touch with my inner being. I thought about Gord. I didn't want to have an inner *being.* He told me he has affinity with all animals, even rats, even ants and moths. He left a bill for one hundred and sixty dollars and said to call him if Grandma sees the rat again. He winked.

I gave Grandma the bill and told her the rat guy had winked and that made her mad. He thinks she doesn't know what a rat looks like? She said not to tell Mom about the rat or the bill because she'd say it was Grandma's medication making her bonkers. Your mom wants me to use essential oils, she said. Have you heard of them? Of course not. They're not real. The rat is real. Essential oils, my foot.

Mom came home early from rehearsals. She said she was *so exhausted* and also the stage manager was still being weird, and meanwhile the director had said it might be a *liability* to have Mom in the play. Also, he said that they might cancel the play altogether because the government was threatening to cut their funding if they kept producing Antifa plays. She went to her room and slammed the door shut.

Grandma and I sat at the dining room table. Grandma was thinking. She crossed her arms and rested them on top of her giant boobs which is like a shelf the size of my mini-Casio. She has so many brown splotches on her arms. It looks like they're joining together to create a whole new skin. She made her face go small. Onward to battle. She dropped her hearing aid batteries on the floor but she didn't notice. When I was crawling around looking for them she told me that she had a friend named Emiliano Zapata who said it was better to die on your feet than to live on your knees.

I said very funny and she patted me on my head and said I was a good kid.

All right, school at home, said Grandma. First, the Sudoku. I'll time you. Have you had a BM? I didn't answer. She said if you bring forth what is within you it will save you. If you do not bring forth what is within you, it will destroy you. That's the gospel of Thomas. She laughed so hard I was one second away from having to Heimlich her. Yes, I said. I did, Grandma, okay? Stop choking! I had a BM! I was trying to save her life. She said okay, good. Begin! There were little bubbles of spit at the corners of her mouth. She wiped them off and said hooooooo. Sudoku was the first class of the day. Actually, the first class was Poached Egg. Grandma showed me *a blood egg.* She threw it away and used a different one that didn't have blood in it. After the egg there was Sudoku and Grandma taught me some Latin medical terms. Then we analyzed our dreams. I told her my dream of trampolines being everywhere outside, all connected, so we can bounce to work, to school, to rehearsal, everywhere. Grandma's face got smaller as she thought. Her forehead was puckered. Well, what do you think that means, Swiv?

How the hell should I know? I told her. I

just dream 'em.

Grandma and I played catch sitting down. She has a special rubber ball with little spikes on it. She also has a rubber elastic thing that she's supposed to exercise her hands with by stretching it out, but she threw it into her laundry basket with her breathing machine. She hates it. She sawed a whodunnit into three parts with a bread knife because it's easier to hold like that when her arthritis is bad. That was one Math Class — for me to make all the parts of her sawed-up book have the same number of pages. Don't tell Mom, she said. Grandma had already sawed Mom's *The Anatomy of Melancholy* into six parts because it was huge — that was seventy-two pages for each part not including all the pages of notes at the end which she didn't want. She hid the parts in her laundry basket so Mom wouldn't find out. Grandma hopes that Mom never remembers that she had that book in the first place or goes looking for it, but even if she did she wouldn't find it because I do Grandma's laundry. Better not be reading one of the sections when Mom's around, I told her. Grandma and I re-enacted what that would be. I played the role of Mom. Hey, I said. Is that one-sixth of my *Anatomy of Melancholy*?

Nooooo, said Grandma. It's a leaflet from the hospital. No! I said. You chopped up my *Anatomy of Melancholy*! How could you? It was easy, said Grandma. I used the bread knife. Seriously, Grandma, I said, you better not let her see you reading it. I'm not gonna read a book called *The Anatomy of Melancholy,* said Grandma, you've gotta be kidding me!

Math Class was also about figuring out when Grandma and I would meet on the height chart that we wrote on the door between the kitchen and the dining room. If I'm 5'1' now, said Grandma, and you're 4'5', and if you're growing at the rate of two and a half inches per year and I'm shrinking at the rate of one quarter of an inch per year, then when do we meet on the chart? Three years and four months, I said. Could be! said Grandma. Who knows, we'll find out! In real school you'd know if I was right or not, I told her. It's inexact, she said. This is actually a lesson in patience, not math, because we'll have to wait to find out. We'll keep checking! We need things to look forward to. Would you like to wear my clothes when we're the same size? Oh, look at the expression of horror on your face! You don't like my snazzy track suit? It's velour! Hahahahaha. Fun and games!

Next class was Boggle. First Real Boggle and then Fake Boggle which is when we make our own words from the letters, words that aren't real words, and we tell each other what they mean in under a minute. Grandma writes them all down. She told me what a cipher key was. Then we had Fast Cooking. We made Survival Casserole and 1-2-3-4 Cake in sixteen minutes, which was a record. Grandma recorded it, which for her means writing it down on paper. Grandma likes to do everything fast. When she wants to leave and Mom and I aren't ready she yells, Bus is loading in lane seven! Mom gets so mad when Grandma takes off down the sidewalk before Mom can get her shoes on to help her. Once, in the middle of a blizzard, Grandma was *adamant* about going to her book club because they were doing Euripides who is a *peer* of Grandma's. She said they're the same age and shared a desk at school. Back then she was 5'7' and Euripides was jealous of her. She had to help him with everything because he was a dreamer. She took off to book club before me or Mom could catch her. We waited at home steaming mad because it was a very serious blizzard and Grandma was *a fucking nutbar* for going out in that weather. She came back hours and hours later like *fucking*

Achilles returning from Troy. Mom was so mad she didn't help Grandma off with her winter boots. Grandma was triumphant. Her face was all red and she was covered in snow. She told us she got to the streetcar stop on the icy streets by throwing down her woolen hat for traction and stepping on it and then picking it up and throwing it down again, stepping on it, and so on and so on until she got to the stop and then she told some very handsome guys standing there to push her onto the streetcar and there you go, she made it to Euripides. How did you get back? I asked her. Mom was already off slamming things around in another room. She didn't want to hear how Grandma got back. I just did it the same way! said Grandma. I have not been in the company of so many handsome men in quite some time! Unless you count that last ambulance ride. They just love to help me! We got you, they say. You're good. *We got you.* Isn't that *wonderful?*

Next class was Ancient History (Made Modern). Grandma told me that when she was born her mother was so sick and tired she thought she was going to die, so she left the hospital and went home, what else could she do? She left Grandma in the hospital to be taken care of by the nurses. That's why

65

Grandma wanted to become a nurse later. They loved Grandma and fought over who got to hold her. Grandma's mom had fourteen other kids at home to take care of so she got well again and then *sent for Grandma.* When Grandma turned eight her dad gave her a job. When the house started filling up with smoke she had to run downstairs and shovel coal. She slept in the hallway and had a good vantage point for detecting the smoke. When she was eight her parents had taken her out of their bed and put her in a crib in that hallway because she was small for her age and because they had run out of beds and bedrooms. Grandma was nimble enough to leap right out of the crib at the first hint of smoke. The rest of the family could *slumber* on obliviously while little Grandma shovelled the coal and saved them all from suffocating in their sleep. Her parents loved her very much. Her father was a *rogue* who became a rich lumberman and her mother was *pious* and had been a thirteen-year-old maid in the city and was stood up at the altar twice by Grandma's dad because he liked being in the bush with the men and didn't know if he was ready to settle down and have fifteen children with a poor maid. He'd really wanted to marry a different lady but that lady's brothers said no way, she couldn't marry that wild lumberjack. Then that other woman had an accident and *became a different person.* Grandma's father built their house with the strongest wood, oak, to prevent Grandma's older brothers from destroying it with their *roughhousing.* They literally swung from the rafters and threw themselves down staircases and slammed their bodies against the walls all the time. They lived in the town on the main street next to the lumberyard. When Grandma went to play with her friends who lived on farms they teased her for not knowing how to extract fluids from animals or kill them. One of them forced Grandma to cut the head off a chicken. Then they ate that chicken for dinner and chased Grandma home, waving the chicken's feet and head at her. Grandma turned around on the gravel road and told them all to go to hell, that was no way to treat a guest. When she got home she was in trouble with Willit Braun for telling the farm kids to go to hell but her father told Willit Braun to stop being a hypocrite. Kids will be kids. Get down from your pulpit. Grandma's dad shooed Willit Braun off the porch and gave Grandma a Cuban Lunch chocolate bar he'd bought in the city. Every time he came back from the city he had a Cuban Lunch for her. And one time a mug that said *Fino alla fine.*

When Grandma's dad died, her brothers took over everything and left the sisters in the dirt. They even stole the house that was supposed to go to the girls. They made all the workers in the factory pray together every ninety minutes and promise God they wouldn't form a union. Grandma was fifteen years old. Her brothers sent her away to Omaha, Nebraska to study the Bible and work as a live-in maid for *an American family.* They wanted her to find a husband or become a missionary so she'd be taken care of by someone other than them. That's patriarchy, Swiv, make a note. I waved my phone at her.

One time, Grandma's brother's wife felt very guilty about randomly having married into all the family money while the *legitimate heirs,* Grandma and her sisters, had none of the family money, so she wrote Grandma a cheque for twenty thousand dollars. Grandma *beat a fast track* to the bank to cash it before her nephew could put a stop payment on the cheque. Later he told Grandma that his mom, her brother's wife, was not in her right mind when she gave Grandma that cheque. Whenever she was feeling generous her family called her crazy. Grandma used the money to pay off a bunch of loans and to buy a screen door so she could feel the evening breeze without getting eaten alive by mosquitoes after schlepping around all day in the blazing hot prairie sun. All her life she had wanted a screen door. A few years before that she had asked her nephews for a screen door, at cost, from the family business, but her nephews said no, that was impossible because if they gave Grandma a screen door, at cost, they'd have to give all their aunts a screen door, at cost, and where would that all end? Also, the nephews said they made *high-end* products and that probably wouldn't be suitable for Grandma. What on earth does that mean? Grandma asked me.

Grandma was on her Gazelle as she was talking about this. I have a mental image, she said. She told me about one day when she was young and she was walking down the street. She was freezing to death. It was thirty below. The wind was blowing hard. Nobody else was outside. This was in her town. She doesn't know why she was walking around outside when it was so cold and the wind was blowing so hard. I asked her if she'd been sad. She was still huffing and puffing on her Gazelle. She said maybe,

69

maybe not. Maybe she'd been sent on an errand that day. She was walking and freezing. She was mad, she remembered suddenly. She was mad, not sad. There was no errand. Then she saw three people walking towards her in the swirling snow. They had to get close to her before she could really see them. They were an old grandma and her two grandsons. The old grandma had a lit cigarette sticking straight out of her mouth. It wasn't dangling. The little boys were wearing one mitten each. They held popsicles in their other hands, the ones without mittens on them. They were licking their popsicles. And they were all happy. They were all smiling. It was minus thirty degrees. The wind was howling. It was a prairie blizzard. Nobody was around. Grandma got close to them on the sidewalk. The old grandma said to Grandma, who was young then and not a grandma, Not too bad out, eh? Her cigarette stuck straight out of her mouth even when she talked.

I asked Grandma why she'd had that memory right now. Not too bad out, eh? said Grandma. She said she often had that memory. It was just a regular flash.

Mom came out of her room, crying. She went into Grandma's bedroom with

70

Grandma and they shut the door. I put water on to boil for the conchigliettes. Then Mom came out of the bedroom and asked me if I wanted to go to the card shop with her and pick out a notebook for me and a card for the stage manager to say she was sorry for the Netflix thing. Grandma came shuffling along behind her and said she'd finish making dinner.

Mom blew another gasket at the card shop. I already knew she was mad because she called the innocent squirrels on the deck assholes. Fuck off, jerks! They had to kamikaze off the railing into the neighbour's yard to escape from Mom. Wallenda Brothers, said Mom. They're just squirrels, I said. Mom doesn't care what they are. They're mocking little vengeful creeps. They cause fires. We waited in a line-up at the cash register for twenty minutes which Mom spent writing her message in the card. When we finally got to the checkout to pay, Mom used the surface of the counter to quickly address the envelope and the shop owner guy with *the gleaming incisors* who was standing behind the counter asked me and Mom to please move away from the counter so that he could help ring out the other customers. Mom said she was just addressing the envelope, it would take her five seconds and then he could go on facilitating capitalism. The shop owner said they liked to *encourage* their customers to take the cards *home* and then to take their time to do something *creative* with them. Then Mom really started to take her time addressing and licking the envelope and sticking a stamp on it. When she was finished she looked around and said the only creative thing she could see in that *pale, tasteful* little shop was the markup on the cheesy inventory they carried and maybe he should *create* a space where paying customers feel welcome to address their envelopes, the ones purchased at a creative markup price from the store itself, and not expect people to buy a goddamn card and envelope, go home, read *The Artist's Way,* get inspired, be creative with a cute message, go back out, find a goddamn mailbox that hasn't been knocked over by meth-heads, drop the thing in the slot, slip three times on the ice, break your tailbone and go home again to find cops waiting in every fucking corner and watching your every fucking move through the fucking modern thermostats. The shop owner said that was an incredibly interesting idea, he'd consider it, but for now he had customers to take care of. Mom said that when the shop owner opened his mouth it was like when that kid in *Close Encounters of the Third Kind* opens the door to the aliens and is almost blinded.

I pulled Mom by the hand and told the shop owner very quietly that Mom was pregnant. Mom shouted, This is not about being pregnant! She tried to rip the tinkling thing off the door when we left. Everybody was quiet in the card shop. Mom huffed and puffed all the way home. She couldn't stand how tasteful the shop was and how white the shop owner's teeth were. I started to say, And you really hate modern thermostats, don't you? But by then Mom was off in a world of her own, softly growling and trying to lower her heart rate with her precious Alexander technique.

Grandma had the conchigliettes ready for us, with her Guatemalan woven placemats and candlelight and special blue glass candleholders that Auntie Momo had given her two weeks before she died. Grandma tried to get Mom to relax by making her laugh or at least move her lips into the shape of a smile. She asked Mom if she knew about positions to have sex in when you're pregnant. Her friend Wilda said her daughter was teaching a pre-natal course at the Y and it was just amazing what the body could do and *accommodate.* Mom said oh god,

Mom. Who am I having sex with? Grandma said no, of course not, she knew that, but just in general. She started listing positions that were comfortable to have sex in. Stop! I said. Ho! said Grandma. Why not talk about this? I said, Because it's not funny. Funny! said Grandma. It's not supposed to be funny! Mom sat with her arms crossed. Her head was tipped way over to the right. Okay, said Grandma. You want Grandmas to be funny history lessons all the time, not the Kama Sutra. Well, I had one dress made out of branches to last me for eighteen years and no shoes or cellphone when I was your age, Swiv. Is that better? When Euripides, Zapata, McClung and I were young we had to eat trees and drink our own urine to survive. Luckily we had two sets of sharp teeth, like sharks. Our grandparents *were* sharks. We had to visit them at Christmas and Easter underwater. They loved us so much. They made us eat so much. They didn't speak English. They were so slippery and it was hard to hug them goodbye. We'd laugh and laugh about how slippery Grandma and Grandpa were. People hibernated back then, not just bears. We all fell asleep in the fall from late October to early April.

No! I said. That's not even true. We had

gills, said Grandma. Mom interrupted. Grandma and I smiled because we were so happy Mom was finally saying something. Why don't you tell her about the time you stole a car, she said.

Ah! said Grandma. Now we're talking turkey. I stole a car once accidentally from the Penner Foods parking lot and when I called Sobering the cop to report it, he asked me if I planned to return it. I said yeah and he said okay, good, not a problem. I told him that before I returned it I'd just quickly use it to run a few errands around town. Yeah, that should be fine, he said. Then I might drive to the city and catch a movie, I told him. Hmmmm, well, he said, that oughta be okay. And then, I said, it'll be late so I might just drive home and return it in the morning, if that's okay. Sure, said Sobering, sounds good. The real owner of the car will be asleep anyway. Oh, I said, I just remembered that tomorrow morning I've got a driving test. I had my driver's license taken away six months ago for stunt driving and I have to re-do the test to get it back. Oh, said Sobering, right, you better do that first. You don't want to be driving without a valid license.

Grandma was in *fine fettle.* She'd had a little bit of the Canadian rum from the Italian bottle but believe it or not for once she didn't talk about the doctors murdering everyone. She got so carried away that she forgot to take her meds after dinner. Then she remembered. Her pill box was annoying her because the plastic lid of one of the days of the week was broken and pills kept falling out of it. Bombs away, Swiv! She yelled at me while I crawled around under the table looking for them. This one is tiny, white and round! This one is oblong and pink, with an indentation in the middle! This one is I don't know what, it's a pill! And don't tell me it's time for the blister packs! After her pills, Grandma made me go to her bedroom and get a box of photos. She showed me and Mom a photo of her old Russian ancestors. None of them were smiling. It looked like they were arranging themselves to be executed. Grandma said the names of each of them and how they were related to us. Mom was getting bored and texting with someone but also lifting her head quickly in between texts to look at the picture for one second. This one with his hand on the old woman's shoulder is her son, said Grandma. He's old, too. The old woman was the only person sitting in a chair. The rest of them all stood around her or behind her. This young girl with her hand on the old woman's other shoulder became my grandmother, said Grandma. At the end of her life she was enormous. We used to float around together on Falcon Lake. I really loved her. This boy here had problems with his blood. And look at the old woman in the chair, said Grandma. I poked Mom so she'd stop texting and look. She's dead, said Grandma. What do you mean? I said. Mom said, Let me see that, and she picked up the photo album and held it closely to her face. Well, she's just dead! said Grandma. That's how it was done then. Photos were forbidden but sometimes, especially after somebody had died, people regretted that they had no picture to remember them by, so they quickly got a photographer to come and take a picture before the person was buried.

Mom and Grandma got talking about other things and the whole time they were talking the photo album lay open on the table with the picture of the dead woman. I tried not to look at it but I couldn't stop myself. Mom and Grandma didn't care. They made jokes about it. They didn't look at it while they talked. I tried to make the times I didn't look at the picture longer and longer. I counted seconds. But I kept having to look. I looked at the young girl who was *Grandma's grandma*! Her hand was on a dead person.

4.

This morning I went downstairs and found Grandma lying on the kitchen floor. She was singing. Grandma! I shouted it. Oh! said Grandma. Good morning, sunshine! What are you doing! I said. Just resting, she said. No! I yelled again. Grandma! What are you doing? She laughed. She said hooooooo. I was helping her up. What happened! I said. She said, na oba, jeepers creepers, where'd you get them peepers. I was mad. Cool your jets! said Grandma. Nothing happened! Nuscht! I just fell. Oba! Not a problem, not a problem. I helped Grandma walk to her chair and sit down properly. She was trying to breathe and laugh and talk.

What happened is that the wheel on her walker came off, and so she fell. Usually she doesn't need her walker but today she needed it because of her *ridiculous foot business.* She didn't fall hard. She fell in slow motion, but she couldn't get back up. She tried to but she couldn't. She decided to pass the time by singing hymns in her secret language. She sang a hymn about the Lord. The translation was: I can't take another step without you, Lord. Then she realized that was literally true and she started laughing and couldn't stop. It was the funniest thing that had happened to her in years, since the time she got stuck between the pews in St. Patrick's Cathedral, and not counting being hazed at nursing school. She could see the clock on the stove. It was really early, and me and Mom were still sleeping. She decided to call out my name and Mom's name every fifteen minutes. We didn't hear her. She had no air to shout. She only had enough air to sing and laugh.

Today I was Grandma's human walker. She stood behind me with her hands on my shoulders and we shuffled slowly from room to room. Conga line! said Grandma. It's just one of those things. I called Mario and he's going to come here and fix her wheel. He said he's going to bring some of Joe's fresh corn for us. After breakfast and dropping pills and showering and shuffling around Grandma was so tired she needed to lie down for a bit. I lay down beside her. I squeezed in between her and a bunch of her books and clothes that are always on her bed and never move an inch, even when she's sleeping in bed next to them. Grandma uses an obituary of Auntie Momo as her bookmarker. It's getting ragged. Grandma wants me to laminate it for her. We lay in bed and watched *Call the Midwife.* Grandma told me about different types of difficult births that she had *scrubbed for* when she was a nurse. We were quiet together, holding hands and breathing.

Why is Mom so weird? I asked Grandma. She had fallen asleep. Weird? she said, after a minute. She put on her glasses. Well, let's see. Is it because of Gord? I asked her. No, no, said Grandma. Well, maybe. Her hormones might be out of whack but that's not really why she's weird, as you say. Gord makes her happy! Really? I said. Very happy, said Grandma. As do you. Grandma moved her hand over my hair. It got caught in a massive tangle and she laughed. She called the tangle an *elflock.* Your mom is fighting on every front, said Grandma. Internally, externally. Eternally, I said. Yes, it would seem so, said Grandma. With your dad being gone and —

But where is he? I asked her. The truth is we don't know, said Grandma. Is he dead? I said. Unlikely, said Grandma. I don't think he is. And your mom is worried about losing her mind, said Grandma. Well, everybody worries about that, especially as one ages, but your Mom is terrified of losing her mind because of what she has inherited. Mom is a fighter on every front, said Grandma. She has to be. And a lover, too! Because of Gord? I asked. Because of everything, said Grandma. She screws around, I said. Perhaaaaaaps, said Grandma, but we can express that in so many different ways. And what difference does it make. Women are punished forever for everything! And her biggest fear is of losing you and Gord. I won't be around forever to take care of you and your dad is MIA for the time being.

I take care of *you*! I said. Ha! said Grandma. That's true, you do. But if your mom gets sick she worries about who will take care of you and Gord. I will! I said. Like the Boxcar Children. You could do it, said Grandma. You definitely have what it takes. But it might not be *ideal.* Yeah, I said. I'd rather raise Gord on a boat than a boxcar without wheels so we could actually get to places and ideally travel the world. Mom is afraid of *losing her mind* and killing herself but Grandma says she's nowhere near losing her mind and killing herself. There's stress, said Grandma. And fear and anxiety and rage. These are normal things. Normal, normal, normal. And then there's mental illness. That's a whole other kettle of fish. Whoa. Grandpa and Auntie Momo killed themselves, and your dad is somewhere else, those things are true, said Grandma. But *we're* here! We are all here now. Then Grandma recited a poem or something. "In the long shadows of their misdeeds we are here fighting for the light of the world." But in fact, she said, their suicides weren't *misdeeds.* She talked about that. While she talked she tried to untangle the knot in my hair gently. She picked up one of the books on her bed. It was a thin book so she hadn't needed to saw it into pieces. Let's see, let's see, let's see, she said. Where is that? Then she found it and read: "He reached out a hand. Was it really raining still? No, it wasn't. The sky spread itself unevenly and thinly as if it could open whenever the time came. Sparrows appeared on the wires, sat shaking the rain off. Yes, the world was . . . however it wanted to be. One way or the other, it wasn't to be counted upon. It pleased itself. Not much point in having special wishes, as far as the world went, that was clear. So long as one could be alive, take part in it. And that's what he was doing."

Grandma closed the book and put it next to her on the immovable pile on her bed. Isn't that wonderful? she said. I nodded. We didn't talk. I didn't know if it was wonderful. I lay next to Grandma with my head half on her arm and half on her chest. She smelled like a coconut. I thought about what Grandma had told me. *What she has inherited.* We watched three episodes of *Call the Midwife* and Grandma fell asleep during the second one. Her snoring was louder than the screaming mother and screaming baby combined.

Mom came home late from rehearsal and she and Grandma whispered together in Grandma's room.

5.

Today when I woke up, Mom was already gone, but she'd left me a note saying she was sorry for being such a shitty mother, that she loved me so much and that things would get better. But what things? She wrote words in quotation marks that said, "It is important to fail at mothering or else your child will not pass from illusion to reality: the mother teaches the child to handle frustration by being one." Then she drew a smiley face and a heart and the words Ha! Ha! And she added a P.S. that said, That's D.W. Winnicott's concept of the "good enough mother." She wrote, Love, Mom.

I ran downstairs to show the letter to Grandma. She's gonna kill herself! I said. Grandma said honey, honey, she's *not* going to kill herself. She's telling you she's sorry for being weird, as you say, and that she loves you so much. In fact she'll be home very soon. She's just gone out to get coffee filters.

Yesterday Mom brought home Raptors jerseys for me and Grandma. We tried them on and played catch for ten minutes with Grandma's exercise ball. Grandma said hoooooo, I'm Larry Bird, who are you? I'm worried she's starting to get demented *and* Mom is gonna kill herself. Grandma's leg really hurts right below the knee and she doesn't know why, it's a new thing. She checked to make sure she had enough *bullets* in her purse so she can go out to play cards all day today with her friends. When she swallows her pills she pretends they're tiny soldiers sent off to fight the pain and sometimes she holds them up and says to them, thank you for your service, lest we forget, and then she swallows them and says *play ball*! There's a bathroom right next to where she and her friends play games all day, she said. So that's good. She said she's always had a good bladder, not like her sister-in-law Henrietta with her dodgy waterworks who always had to know where the washrooms were in Panama City because there were very, very few public washrooms there. Grandma could go all day without having to use the washroom. You were the winner! I said. Grandma said there are no winners or losers when it comes to bladder control.

Grandma's friends came to pick her up and they all hugged and laughed at the door and gave me a bag of buns. They spoke their secret language with each other. They were in *cahoots.* Grandma winked at me as if to say relax, don't worry, everything is ridiculous!

When she was gone I felt frozen, like a bug in amber, and I didn't know what to do.

I sat on the stairs and thought. I wrote the word *freewheelin'* on my jeans in two parts on the spaces above my knees. *Free* was bigger than *wheelin'.* I should have measured it out. Grandma says to keep everything freewheelin'. But how?

Then Mom came *bursting* through the door. Oh no, scorched earth. But she was happy! She was smiling and stomping her feet. She acted as though being alive was *obvious.* Maybe she wasn't gonna kill herself after all! She asked me what I was doing. Just sitting here on the stairs? she asked. And writing and thinking, I said. Let's go, she said. She pulled me up off the stairs. She hugged me. She asked me if I'd been crying. Obviously not! I said. Have you? She laughed and then whoosh! She had me by the hand. We were out the door. *Critical interventions!* she shouted. I looked around to see if anyone had heard her. The smoking guy next door smiled. He started singing the song he always sings, about not wanting to go to rehab. Me and Mom walked and walked. We passed the cop parked on the Walnut Street side. I told her not to do anything or say anything. She said no, no, no, I won't, but believe it or not she did do something, I don't know what, but the cop smiled and nodded like *okay, crazy mother lady.* Mom could write her own book about taking care of children if all you have to do is make them frustrated so they get used to reality. Then we walked through the park, past the dogs in the off-leash pit, and then around past the outdoor market where we bought cookies and then down to the lake where we bought hot dogs and then back past the roti place which was packed and all the way downtown where we bought Nutella crepes and she did most of the talking. She wanted to tell me things about herself. She wanted me to know she wasn't going to kill herself. Did Grandma tell you to tell me that? I asked her. Not exactly, she said. She told me you were worried about it. Well, are you? I asked her. Going to kill myself? she said. I didn't nod or say anything. I didn't want to *talk* about it. I just wanted her to say no. No! she said. Never. Well, maybe when I'm old and in horrific pain with no end in sight, she said. You mean like Grandma? Now I was worried again! Grandma will kill herself! No! said Mom. Not like Grandma. She's going the assisted dying route, I said. With all her friends. Listen, said Mom. People die. I sighed and slumped over. I know that! I said. I already know that!

Mom talked about fighting. She said if she wasn't fighting she was dying. And that she has to fight to feel alive and to balance things out. So she keeps fighting. She said we're all fighters, our whole family. Even the dead ones. They fought the hardest. She said she sometimes felt haunted by Grandpa and Auntie Momo. She thought about their last minutes and seconds and about what they were thinking and then about their bodies being in pieces and what if they didn't die right away. The worst thing is that they were alone. Auntie Momo had wanted Mom to write her letters but Mom didn't. She just sent e-mails. Why didn't she write letters? That's another one of her fights. She said she replaces those images in her head with pictures of me and Gord, even though Gord doesn't exist yet. She said what makes a tragedy bearable *and* unbearable is the same thing — which is that life goes on. She told me she says things to herself like, my suffering is the world's suffering. My joy is the world's joy. She just went on and on. She said part of fighting is saying things to yourself. While she walked and talked she tilted her head way over to one side and counted to thirty and then moved it way over to the other side and counted to thirty. She said she was trying to create space between her vertebrae.

We sat on a bench in the park and watched two men play tennis. Mom said she hated this new thing called mini-tennis. It's where the people playing tennis warm up by hitting the ball back and forth in the small area first and then gradually move back so that they're using the full court. Mom just hates that so much. It looks bad, she said. It's ridiculous. It's just so timid! If you're going to play a game of tennis then play it properly and warm up properly with the full court. Mom used to play tennis all the time with Auntie Momo. That's the way to play tennis, she said. The way we did it.

Mom said sometimes she and Auntie Momo played doubles with two guys from Lundar. They were the same age as Auntie Momo. Eighteen. Mom was twelve. One day one of the guys came to the tennis court to say they couldn't play doubles because his doubles partner was in jail. He had been stopped for speeding on the number six highway on the way to Eriksdale. He had a lot of stress in his life. I guess he freaked out, said Mom. He'd grabbed the Mountie's baton and hit him over the head. Then he'd stolen the Mountie's gun. Then he'd stolen the Mountie's unmarked vehicle. And then he took off to see his mom. Hmmm, I said. Mom said yeah. She was quiet. Then she said but I get it, I *get* it. Eventually the guy got out of jail, said Mom, and they played doubles again for a while until they all . . . She moved her hands around. Scattered, she said. I asked if they were still friends and Mom said yeah, except that she was pretty sure he'd died. Then how can you be friends! I said. She said you can be friends with dead people. Swiv, she said, we need to embrace our humanity.

Go ahead! I said. (Mom loves to hate things *or* embrace things.) I don't even know what you mean. Mom was going to explain things to me but *fate intervened* and I was saved from having to embrace anything.

What happened is we met a friend of Mom's who is a director. Mom said oh god, don't look now. Fucking kill me. I looked and saw a tall guy come walking towards us. Mom tried not to embrace him but he bent down and hugged *her* so then out of politeness she hugged *him* for under one second and just with one arm barely touching him. She pointed at me and said, this is my daughter, Swiv. I waved. He said, Oh! I thought you'd say son. Mom and I looked at him. Pleasure, he said. He nodded at me. Mom asked him how he was and he said he was involved in an epic struggle with his demons. Mom burst out laughing and said really? Wow! He said yes, more and more as I get older I'm finding evidence that supports the fact that I'm a tragic character. Mom laughed again. The director looked confused. He said, It's not funny, really, it's painful. Mom couldn't stop laughing. Then I started laughing a bit too. The director frowned and looked away, down towards the far end of the park towards the off-leash pit. Mom said she was sorry. The director said it was fine. He was trying to smile. Finally he left and Mom sat back down on the bench and watched him disappear. When he was far enough away Mom said oh my *god,* what a douchepetard. She told me he had touched her all over — and she means *all* over — during one rehearsal when he was trying to show her how to *simulate love-making.* She said he's *banged every young actress in town* and *super talks down to everyone.* Mom said we can't afford therapy anymore even with the sliding scale and even with giving the therapist free tickets to the theatre because doucherockets like the tall director aren't giving her roles anymore because she's too old and because of Gord and also because he knows she's got his fucking number. Now she has to audition for fucking tooth-whitening commercials.

But where's Dad? I asked her. She said a bunch of things but basically she doesn't know.

Of course, you already know where you are, unless you were kidnapped and taken somewhere with a blindfold and spun around three times. Grandma told me that everything she was taught in her dumb town to be true turned out to be lies. And when you figure that out you have to start all over again.

We sat on the bench watching the timid wankers play mini-tennis. People with tennis rackets sat beside us waiting for them to finish. Mom shouted at the mini-tennis players. Hey! If you're not gonna use the whole court let someone else use it! Go play in your back yard! The mini-tennis guys looked at her. Mom pointed at the people waiting on the bench with their rackets. The people waiting said oh, it's okay, it's okay. Mom grumbled away. I was dying. I said in a low voice, "More and more as I get older I'm realizing that" — then Mom laughed and laughed and forgot about her commitment to harassing the mini-tennis players. She told me she thinks I should have more friends, or at least one friend. I slumped over again and said, I have friends! You said friends could be dead! What dead friends do you have, she said. She asked me if I would consider returning to school. Wouldn't it be nice to see your living friends? I told Mom about King of the Castle. I told her I was obsessed with being King of the Castle. I fought everybody, even grade six boys *tooth and nail* to be King of the Castle. I bled every recess and all my clothes got ripped but I won and I like my clothes like that and it was worth it. Mom said congratulations, that was definitely a fight, but not exactly the kind of fight she was talking about. That's a lonely position to be in, isn't it? she asked me. I hate that therapy voice she gets but I was happy when she said the question was *rhetorical* which means I didn't have to answer. I wished every question in the world was rhetorical. She talked about her big panic attack, the one that happened the night after Grandpa died, when I was a baby. She woke up and couldn't breathe and her chest hurt and she thought she was having a heart attack and was going to die. She didn't want to also die because that would be *too much for Swiv to handle.* Two deaths in two days. Plus she didn't want to wake you up because there was no point to that. She and you couldn't both go to the hospital and leave me alone because I was a baby. And besides she didn't want *anyone* to know she was dying. She drove by herself to the hospital in the middle of the night and the people there said oh, c'mon in. She told them she thought she was dying and they asked her if she'd had any stress in her life lately. They told her she was young and looked very healthy. She told them about Grandpa and they said oh, that is stressful. They checked her out to make sure she wasn't dying. They said she'd have to stay there for a few more hours so they could do the tests again. She said no, she had to get back home and into bed before you and I woke up and noticed she wasn't there.

I can't believe it! I said. I didn't know you did that! You really pulled a fast one! Mom said yeah, she had managed to almost die and then not die without a single person finding out. I said, Wow! I was impressed by that. But it was a lonely time, she said. She said that looking back on it, she felt sorry for her almost-dying, terrified self doing that all alone, sneaking off to the hospital and not telling anyone. She said there were fights and then there were fights. She said it was like me playing King of the Castle at school. (I don't *play* King of the Castle.) Lonely. She told me about another time she'd driven herself to the hospital. It was the night I was born. The reason she knew I was going to be born was because she went to the bathroom in the night and there was a blob of blood-streaked mucus on her panties. That's how you announced your imminent arrival, Swiv! With a blob of mucus in my underwear! Ha! Sexy, right? We were still on the bench *in public* sitting next to the waiting tennis players when she said this. She told me she'd driven to the hospital by herself again because when she told you she was in labour you barely woke up and just moaned oh god, or something not encouraging like that, and it made her really fucking mad. So she went alone to the hospital and even parallel parked in the darkness with her giant stomach. The nurses said she was seven centimetres dilated. She held her hands apart to show me. This much, she said. That's disgusting! I said. You drove a car like that? With this gigantic hole? The point is, she said, that again looking back that was a lonely thing to do. It was a kind of fight, maybe, she said. Like she was saying fuck you, bro, if it's not worth it to wake up for the arrival of your fucking baby after I've already told you I've got mucus in my underwear then I'm going without you! But that's not the kind of fight we need. Look at the Raptors, she said. She stood up and started walking. We need teams. We need others to fight alongside us. She said the reason the Raptors are so good is because they're collectively trying to win, not a single one of them just trying to break personal records or up his stats or whatever. Lonely fights are the worst, she said. She'd rather lose a lonely fight. She'd rather join a losing team than win a lonely fight.

I slumped while we walked so she'd know she could stop talking now! She always uses personal anecdotes in her lectures to me and I already get it! She said lonely fights reminded her of when she was in grade seven and a prison guard came and screamed at her entire class for an hour to stay out of prison. Exactly! I said. Even though I didn't know what she was talking about. Also, Grandma told me that there were one or two Raptors who were more concerned about individual stats but Mom doesn't know that. We held hands on the way home. She put my hand on her stomach to feel Gord. She asked me if I wanted to tell Gord something — which was so stupid. Like maybe if I was two years old. *Swiv, say Hi Gord!* She told me when she was a really little kid she'd ask Grandma, Hey what's for supper? I'm starving to death! And Grandma was always super busy working or talking on the phone with her friends so she'd say, Hey here's a couple of bucks, go to Pete's Inn for a hamburger! Then Mom would walk by herself to Pete's Inn on Main Street in their *fascist little shit town* and sit all by herself in this giant red leatherette booth and order one plain hamburger with nothing on it except ketchup, and an Orange Crush. She'd still have money left over for a tip and an Oh Henry! bar for dessert that she would eat slowly while she walked home and often when she got home Grandma would still be on the phone *whooping it up.* I asked Mom if that was a lonely fight and she said no, it was cool, she loved it, as long as she didn't bump into Willit Braun. She'd rather go out of her way and walk a hundred miles or even crawl a hundred miles or even crawl a hundred miles with a four-hundred-pound wild animal on her back than bump into Willit Braun. What about five hundred miles with a killer shark clamped onto your head with its teeth so you couldn't even see where you were going? Mom said yep, she'd rather walk eight hundred miles with the shark clamped onto her head *and* seven hundred rats gnawing at every part of her skin than bump into Willit Braun. Mom did these stretching exercises while we walked. She called them lunges. She pushed against buildings and light-posts like she was trying to knock them over. She said she was doing it to strengthen her uterus and her *vaginal wall,* and because that's what actors do. Do it with me, Swiv! No! I said. I don't have all that shit. You don't have a uterus and a vaginal wall? she asked me. I walked away while she was pushing as hard as she could against the corner of Nova Era bakery because I don't want to just stand beside her while she does weird things like I'm in support of it. She was almost lying down, and taking up the whole sidewalk, and people had to go all the way around her.

When we got home Grandma was playing Solitaire on her computer. She was so happy to see us. Oh good, you're home! She slammed the lid down on her computer and stood up beside the table. She began to laugh in the way that means something hilarious had happened to her that day and she was going to tell us what it was as soon as she could stop laughing. We just have to stand there and wait. Sometimes Mom gets impatient and stomps off upstairs and says she'll be back in a minute, which she never is. But today Mom was in a good mood from helping me understand life by frustrating me and she stood beside me and smiled and waited with me for Grandma to stop laughing so she could talk. Finally Grandma said okay, listen, do you know how old my friend Wilda and her husband Dieter are? I shook my head and Mom said, Um, eighty? Older! said Grandma. They're almost *centurions,* for heaven's sake! Then Grandma told us this awful story, that she thought was *a riot,* about arriving with her friends at Wilda and Dieter's place and ringing the doorbell and nobody coming to the door, and then all of them going right in, and still nobody coming to say oh hi, you're here, and then walking further in to the kitchen and hearing moaning which they thought for sure was Wilda or Dieter or both of them simultaneously dying because of their age, and then going into the bedroom and seeing Wilda and Dieter *in flagrante delicto on their love seat.* I said, No! I wasn't sure what I was hearing. Mom said oh my god, that's amazing! *Isn't it?!* said Grandma. That was the last thing I heard.

A little while later Mom knocked on my door and said come and eat! I went downstairs thinking it was safe, but no. Grandma and Mom were still talking about it. Grandma said, Oh good, Swiv, you've joined *the land of the living*! Mom asked Grandma if she remembered this time a million years ago when she had given Mom a big gift basket with champagne and fancy cheese and crackers and flowers and sausage and other things to take with her to that cabin in the woods where she was going to lose her virginity with *whatshisname.* I did, didn't I!? said Grandma. And a card, said Mom. Like sort of a congratulations card with love and best wishes and all that! said Mom. I was sixteen! Can you not talk about this anymore? I said. Nobody better be giving me a gift basket when I'm sixteen. Grandma said, Oh, c'mon, Swiv! It's sex! So what! Big deal! Mom was laughing and putting her head way back. I worried about Gord. You'll miscarry Gord! I said. Mom and Grandma laughed harder. I put a pillow on Mom's stomach and they laughed even harder, like demons. I wanted to punch them both in the face and run away from home. Okay, okay, okay, said Grandma. Swiv, I apologize for upsetting you but — she started laughing again. Oh, c'mon, Swiv, said Mom. It's not a terrible thing, I mean it *was* with whatshisname, but generally it's a beautiful —

Okay! I said. Kill Gord then! Have sex with ancient men! I don't care! You're evil!

Grandma said all right, all right, hoooooo, let's cool it. Let's see. Do you know I'm registered for another Later Life Learning class at the university? Oh good! said Mom. Fake enthusiasm, I said. They were trying too hard to talk about other things. They really had to use all their might not to talk about perverted things. What's the class this time? said Mom. Leonard Cohen, said Grandma. And then believe it or not they started talking about it again! He was a real ladies' man, said Grandma. That's what Muriel said. She knew someone who knew him in his mountaintop phase. Yeah, said Mom, he had a real big, you know, following. He *was* kind of sexy in a way. Like you just kind of knew he'd pay full *and complete* attention to you for twenty-four hours or something, and then you'd never see him again. Grandma said well I wouldn't know about that! Mom said trust me. Then she said hey yeah, when *was* the last time you —

Had *intercourse*? said Grandma. Well, let's see! It certainly wasn't this century! Mom said wow. Grandma said well if I've had intercourse *recently* I sure can't remember it! They were laughing again. There went Gord flying around inside Mom. That was it. They were horrible. They were perverts. They were baby killers. They were obsessed with it. It was an obsession for them, like King of the Castle. I went to Grandma's room and turned her Netflix on and watched a show about a nuclear power station exploding and everybody turning into liquid.

6.

This morning Mom was back to her bad mood. Nothing got broken during the night. Before she left she blew her nose two hundred times and dropped piles of Kleenex everywhere that I picked up with the barbecue tongs and threw away. *I have post-nasal drip and I can't take any of that steroid spray shit cuz of Gord! The body produces one quart of mucus a day!* She left streaks of oregano oil in the kitchen sink from spitting. I told her it takes one second to wash these off and saves me a lot of work! When the streaks get hard I have to get out the green pad and scrub them. Nothing got broken during the night, at least. Did I say that already? I picked up hearing aid batteries and Amish farm pieces and conchigliettes from the kitchen floor. Grandma said good luck, have fun, don't work too hard! I hugged Mom around the waist and whispered I love you to Gord. I squeezed hard. Mom rubbed her snotty nose in my hair. She said don't squeeze me too hard or you'll get sprayed with one entire quart of mucus. All she does with her life is talk about mucus. All Grandma talks about is bowel movements. Then Mom mumbled something else and slammed the front door. Your mom's not really a morning person, said Grandma. She was rubbing Voltaren on her hand. Her veins looked like bulging tubes of blue water like at Splash Mountain. She's never a person! I said. I think she's a twilight person, said Grandma. A dusk person. When all the *foofaraw* of the day is coming to an end. Your mom is a crepuscular person.

Grandma and I had Editorial Meeting. What can I do for you today, Swiv? she asked me. I told her today was the deadline for her letter to Gord assignment. Did she have it? Yes, ma'am, she said. Part of it. I said Grandma, have you ever heard the expression "A deadline is not a suggestion"? Just now! she said. Maybe she'd heard it before but she can't remember things like expressions about deadlines anymore. She had written her letter by hand on lined, yellow paper. Did I ask you for a scroll? I said. Did you steal this from the Museum of Ancient History? Did you rob some Pharaoh? I can't read this!

Oh, c'mon, said Grandma. Knock it off!

I tried to read it. I couldn't. I can't read your chicken-scratching, Grandma! Grandma said our next class would be Penmanship. Penmanship! I said. What the holy hell is *penmanship*? Grandma thought I should run around the block twice to get rid of my yips, but I said not until I'd read her assignment. She grabbed it from me and said she'd read it out loud. I asked Grandma to read it twice. Once for me to listen and another time for me to make notes. Very well! she said. She stood up at the dining room table and cleared her throat. This is what she read.

You are ten weeks inside, the size of a kumquat, a nice dirty-sounding word, your head half the size of your body, your hands covering your heart. Protecting your heart, as though we are able to do that. Beginning to kick. If I can manage to *submit* to the terms of my house arrest you and I will emerge from our confinement at the same time, mid-July. It'll be hot, you'll be slippery with thick white slime and screaming, maybe shitting black tar, as freaked out as you'll ever be, hello precarious world, and I'll be right there, maybe not *right* there, your mother and perhaps even your *pilgering weiter* father will be right there, but I'll be there in the parking lot or in the waiting room or in the cafeteria or some dark cabinet or wherever it is that grandmas are put to wait, and I'll be ready for you, little one, my adorable accomplice. You're a small thing and you must learn to fight.

Thank you, Grandma, I said. And again, please? Grandma cleared her throat and read the letter again. I made notes in my new notebook. When Grandma finished she sat down and looked at me. Well? she said. I asked her to wait a minute while I finished writing my notes. Okay, I said. Thank you. This is an excellent start! I'm curious about a few things, though.

Grandma's body language told me that she was pretending to be worried about what I might say.

First of all, I said, is Gord really the size of a kumquat? And also, what is a kumquat? Also, you don't want to use dirty-sounding words a lot, do you? Because remember, Grandma, this is a letter to a baby. Should you be talking about dirty words? Should you be expressing approval for dirty words in a letter to a baby?

Ah, said Grandma. Hmmm. I'll have a

look at that.

Thank you, I said. Also, perhaps you could *clarify* exactly why the word kumquat is dirty. And, of course, as I mentioned, what it is exactly. Remember your readers, okay, Grandma? In this case, a baby.

Ah, yes, point taken! Will do, thank you, said Grandma.

Oh, and also, re the ten weeks inside, I said. Yes? said Grandma. Is it true that the head is half the size of the body? Well, said Grandma, first of all Gord is now much further along than ten weeks so as time passes the body will grow faster than the head and things will become more proportioned. Whew, I said. Because who wants to give birth to a monster. I imagined Mom yelling, *What the fuck is this? Are you fucking kidding me?* right after they showed Gord to her in the hospital.

Secondly, I said. I looked closely at my notes. I smiled so Grandma wouldn't worry. I appreciate this comparison of house arrest and confinement to Gord being in the womb, but may I ask you a question, Grandma? Of course, of course, said Grandma. Are you under house arrest? I asked. No, no, of course not, said Grandma. Because this is a letter, I said. Usually letters are true. Ah, said Grandma. Yes. You make a good point. They usually are. I think it's okay to exaggerate a bit, I told Grandma, especially if there's *some* truth to what you're saying. Well, said Grandma, in a way I think I was comparing being under house arrest to the process of aging.

I stopped and looked hard at Grandma. She looked hard at me. I blinked a few times. Fair enough, I said. That's justified. Grandma seemed really happy about that. But again, I said, always remember your reader. You don't want to replace clarity with clever comparisons. Yes, said Grandma. She nodded. You are right. Thank you. Because, I said, further on you mention that you and the reader of the letter will emerge from your confinement at the same time. Mid-July. Yes, said Grandma. That's right. But if *your* confinement is, as you explained, the process of aging, which you compare to being under house arrest, and it is also coming to an end in mid-July, then what exactly are you saying? That Gord will be born in mid-July and that *you* will stop aging in mid-July? Which means what exactly?

Grandma smiled at me. She put her hand on mine. Ah, she said. I see what you're getting at. She got up from the table and came around to where I was sitting and put her arms around me. She patted my heart. No,

Swiv, she said, I have no plans of dying in mid-July. Or anytime soon!

I hugged Grandma. I couldn't let go. Finally I had to let go because I knew she needed to sit down and knock some things over and catch her breath. Well, I said, just to wrap things up. I was trying not to cry. How could an editor cry in Editorial Meeting? She passed me the box of Kleenex that was on the dining room table. I blew my nose. I coughed. I like the next sentence of your letter, Grandma. It *is* very, very long and you use the word shitting in it, but —

Grandma interrupted me. I need to remember my reader, she said. Who is a baby.

Yes, I said. Exactly. And lastly, I said, what does this expression mean, the one you said about *the father.* Pilgering weiter, said Grandma. Yeah, I said. What does that mean? What does it sound like to you? asked Grandma. I have no idea! I said. It isn't even a real language! It is a real language, said Grandma. It's just not very common! It's not even written down, I said. It's not real! Things don't have to be written down to be real, said Grandma. It means wandering around from spot to spot. Taking things as they come. Do you notice that the first part of the word looks a bit like the word pilgrim?

Was Grandma trying to tell *me* something

about *you* in *her* letter to *Gord*? All right, Grandma, I said. Excellent work. Like I said, you've made a *tremendous* start. I organized my papers and stood up from the table.

Is it time for Facts? said Grandma.

I looked at my cellphone. Yes! I said. Do you have one?

I do, said Grandma, it's about crocodiles. Cool! I said. I lay across the hassock. I was tired of being an editor. Grandma told me that crocodiles have survived evolution and extinction and all that jazz because they have a characteristic that makes them almost indestructible which is the ability to enter a state similar to a living death. I lay very still and silently on the hassock. After a minute, Grandma said yes, exactly like that.

I leapt up. Surprise! I said. I'm alive.

Grandma said she was mighty grateful for that. She asked me if she'd ever mentioned her old friend Marcus to me. I don't think so, I said, who's he? Is he that guy who fell through the ice on his snowmobile? Marcus Aurelius, said Grandma. He really understood impermanence. I don't want to understand impermanence, I told Grandma. I realize that, she said. But the thing is you *are* in the process of understanding impermanence, whether you want to be or not. We all are.

I got up to boil water for the conchigliettes. I can't lie here forever! I said.

You know Buddhism? said Grandma. No, I don't, I said.

It begins with that young princess living her sheltered life and seeing the four signs. She sees an old woman, she sees a sick woman, she sees a dead woman, she sees a holy woman and she realizes, Hey I'm going to get old, I'm going to get sick, and I'm going to die!

Buddhism is about a princess? I asked Grandma. *Ball Game, Swiv!* I ran to the door. I was so happy to be finished with our conversation. It was the twins Geoffrey and Gretchen from my class. Our teacher thinks we're triplets because we all have the same tangled yellow hair and Nike swooshes under our eyes and torn clothing. The twins don't fight, they're not allowed to, but on the first day of school they said they liked my look and asked me if they could copy it. Our teacher said the blue under our eyes made it look like we were *iron deficient*. We all stood at the door smiling at each other. We had enough iron. Gretchen asked me if I could come out and play and I said yeah as long as Grandma would finish the conchigliettes. Ask her, said Geoffrey. He was whispering. I shouted at Grandma about the conchigliettes and she said yes, go play for heaven's sake! As Bobby Sands, political prisoner of the British, said, *Our revenge will be the laughter of our children*!

Geoffrey and Gretchen knew this bank where we could get free doughnuts if we asked them about retirement planning. We went up to the teller and said we wanted to ask her about retirement planning. She said oh just get lost, the doughnuts are over there on that table. When we walked away she said god, I hate my life.

We played football for a long time. Our team was called the Zombies. We could never die. We tried to get more rips in our clothes. Gretchen was the quarterback and every time we huddled she said it's Scrambled Eggs, or sometimes it was Whoot Whoot which were the names of her two plays. Me or Geoffrey would hut the ball to her and then run super fast in a straight line down the field and then turn hard to the left, which was Whoot Whoot, or if it was Scrambled Eggs we'd just run around like crazy all over the place, wherever we felt like going, waiting for her to throw the ball. After football we sat on the monkey bars and talked. This lady came up to us and said the city was closing the park soon to build a *remand centre.* She said now that the world is ending people are replacing having children with becoming criminals which is why we need more remand centres and fewer parks. We sat on the top bars and looked at her and nodded. She said, Can I ask you something? We said sure. Do I look P-A-L-E? We said no! Do I look ill? We said no, you look great! Do I look P-A-L-E? Nope! Do I look friendly? Yes! Do I look friendly and kindly? Yes! Do I look P-A-L-E? Nope! I look friendly and kindly? Yes. Do I look ill? No!

The lady went over to the garbage bin and looked inside it. She wrapped a giant scarf around and around her head and then she took it off again and wrapped it around her waist. She did jumping jacks. We whispered to each other. We didn't know if she was great or not great. She walked away to where the streetcar stops and told us to have ourselves a fantastic day and God bless us.

We went back to my place. Gretchen screamed when she saw Grandma sleeping in her chair. I think she's dead, she said. No, I said. That's how she looks. Geoffrey and Gretchen never see old people. I put my head on Grandma's chest. It went up and down.

Gotcha! Grandma yelled. She grabbed me and we all screamed.

Let's eat! said Grandma. She talked to Geoffrey and Gretchen about stuff while I set the table with the blue glass candleholders from Auntie Momo and the yellow cloth napkins. I told Geoffrey and Gretchen they had to yell at Grandma for her to hear them. They were too shy at first, but finally everyone was yelling like usual.

When Mom came home after rehearsal she went to her room and cried. Geoffrey and Gretchen went home. Mom turned her humidifier up high so I wouldn't hear her crying but I heard her anyway. I lay down beside her and she smiled and blew her nose four hundred times. She said sorry, sorry, sorry, god I'm just so exhausted, Swiv, don't worry.

Worry about what? I said. Because I wasn't worried until she told me not to worry. What shouldn't I worry about? I asked her.

Anything, she said. Just don't worry about a thing.

I felt my whole body freeze up. I couldn't move it. As if Mom had tucked me into a blanket of worry that was the world's heaviest blanket in the *Guinness Book of World Records.* Do you have your letter? I asked her.

What letter? she said.

Your assignment, I told her. Of the letter. Grandma already handed hers in and they're due.

Mom said oh god, right, yeah, I think so, maybe, let me check my bag, or maybe it's on my computer, hang on, I think I've got it, or maybe I'm not done, actually I don't think I've . . .

I lay beside Mom while she said all those things and more. The truth was there was no letter. I didn't say anything for a long time. Mom rubbed my back as if a massage could be a substitute for a letter. I'm disappointed, I said. Mom said she knew, she was sorry, she knew a deadline is not a suggestion but —

It's just that you're so exhausted, I said. Mom was quiet and we breathed together quietly. We could hear the Raptors game blaring away on Grandma's TV. You know what Swiv, she said, I'm gonna finish tonight. May I please have a one-hour extension? I tapped my chin and squinted at Mom. You're treading on thin ice, my friend, I said. Mom nodded, she knew, she knew. I managed to get out from under the cement blanket of worry and stood up next to the bed. One hour! I said.

I stomped downstairs to watch the Raptors and set the timer on the stove. Grandma asked me what I was timing. Mom, I said. Was it nice seeing your friends? Grandma asked, and I said yeah. Did you have fun? she said. Does it make you want to go back to school? I was getting a rhetorical vibe from her questions. I can't go back to school! I said. I've been suspended! I know, said Grandma, but after your suspension. I don't know, I said. Grandma wanted to talk about it more, but I didn't. We stared at the TV.

The Raptors weren't playing hard. Grandma was mad. She told them, C'mon you guys, wake up and smell the coffee. She said that's a terrible, terrible way to lose, by not trying and not fighting. You play hard to the end, Swiv. To the buzzer. There is no alternative. Do they all have the flu? Then she said she was so disgusted that she couldn't watch anymore and she switched the TV to *Jeopardy!*

One hour was almost up. Just as I was about to go upstairs to tell Mom, I heard her coming down the stairs. She came into the living room pretending to be all nervous and curtsied to me and Grandma and then handed me her pages. She kept her head down and her eyes on the carpet as she handed them to me. My lady, she said. As you requested. I'm grateful to you for the mercy shown. Forgive me. Then she crawled backwards out of the room with Gord hanging down from her stomach and almost scraping the rug. The timer went off. Fun and games! said Grandma. I hid my smile with Mom's pages.

I gave Grandma her seven thousand evening pills. In two days I'd have to get some of her prescriptions renewed at the drugstore. I went into her room and put a thin-rimmed glass of water by her bed and moved her nitro spray closer on the bedside table — but not too close, so she wouldn't knock it off in her sleep. I put her cellphone with my number taped on it beside the bed and made sure it was charged. I went back into the living room to say goodnight to Grandma. I put her nitro patch on the fattest part of her arm to really soak up that TNT. I asked her to drink a glass of water before bed even though I know she wouldn't. She says she gets her water from coffee. I asked her to floss her teeth because it helps prevent heart attacks. She laughed. She said that's rich. She wanted to hug me for a long time. Embrace your humanity, Grandma, I said. I whispered it into her fat. I told her the next day I'd help her shower and we could use Mom's expensive Italian shower gel. Mom wouldn't notice because she was too preoccupied with going insane. Grandma told me she loved me very much.

I went to my room to read Mom's assignment.

Dear Gord,
For now you're a part of me. Your life is dependent on mine. For now your world is tiny, but soon — well, listen — I'm an actor, not a writer. Swiv gave me this assignment, of writing you a letter, but I just don't know what to say. And I've got this deadline . . . I mean, I do know what I want to *tell* you one day, but I don't want to write it down here. Why don't I want to write letters? My sister, your aunt, she's dead, asked me (begged me!) to write letters to her and I didn't. Why didn't I write the fucking letters? I remember reading an interview with a writer once and she said that she was writing *against* death, that the act of writing, or of storytelling, that every time she wrote a story I mean, she was working through her own death. She

119

didn't care about impermanence. She didn't care if anybody read her stories. She just wanted to write them down, to get them out of her. Gord, you're a story inside of me. You're everything, man. Every joy, every sorrow, every joke, every heartbreak, every freedom, every sweetness, every rage, every humiliation, every fight, every serenity, every possibility that has ever existed. Can I keep you inside of me forever? I want to. Just like I'd still like to be inside of my mother! (Grandma. Who I really hope you'll meet, but . . . chemicals are keeping her alive right now, I think.) Well, on some days. Many days. I mean on many days I'd like, still, to be inside of her and not this world. This world, man . . . you have to know who you are. Know you are loved. Know you are strong. I'm not a writer! Remember these words. "They can kill me, but they can't scare me." Your great-grandfather said that. Freedom comes at a cost, Gord. Men who are otherwise sane and respectable will lose their shit when women attempt to set themselves free. They lose perspective and they lose all shame. They will abandon babies and go to Shibuya forever. They will steal your passport and strand you in Albania. They will mock you when you refuse to take your clothes off. They will claim ownership of your work and steal your royalties. They will tell their friends you're crazy and send you Google maps that look like targets with your house circled in the centre as the bullseye. They will demand your wages. They will try to fuck you over every which way from Tuesday. I had a dream last night that I had planned for three interviews to take place at our house in Toronto and I forgot about every one of them. All the interrogators arrived at once. I made an excuse to go to my car, to get something out of the back seat. The interrogators said that while they were waiting they would very quickly repaint my staircase. I ran out of the house. I got behind the wheel and took off, but then found myself in a parking lot and couldn't find my ticket to get out and through the wooden barrier. I decided to smash through it. Instantly a young woman appeared next to me in the front seat. I told her, Well, looks like you're coming with me. Do you want to be my friend? She said no, quickly. There was no pause before her answer. I was devastated and angry and determined, more than ever, to smash through the barrier. Afterwards, careening about on the city streets, I tried to check my e-mail on my cellphone. I couldn't get it to work. I saw the e-mail of everyone I knew, for some reason, but not my own. I handed my phone to the girl, the one who definitely did not want to be my friend, and pleaded with her to fix my phone so that I could see my own e-mail. She grabbed my phone, sneering, pushed one button quickly and handed it back to me. It worked. She was so disdainful. I was so grateful, but troubled.

The cops took me to the hospital in the back of a cruiser and dropped me off at the emergency room and a giant, muscly guy with a whistle around his neck who worked in psych showed me around my new lodgings which included a white room with nothing in it but a drainhole in the middle of the floor. The giant told me that's where I'd go if I misbehaved. Bring it, I said. I turned around to leave and he grabbed my arm and I used my other fist to punch him in the head. Nope, he said, you can't do that. That's exactly the thing you can't do. I managed to squirm away from him and took off down the hallway but an orderly at the end intercepted me with his meal trolley and I plowed right into it and wiped out on the slick of apple juice that spilled in the collision. I knocked myself out when my head hit the floor and woke up wearing a disposable diaper and chained to a bed. What. Ever. They kept me tied up for two days and force-fed me anti-psychotic drugs which fucked up my coordination and made my eyeballs do strange things. I would focus them on something in my room, the wall or the end of the bed, but my vision would go elsewhere. I mean if I was looking at the wall beside the window, for instance, I was *seeing* the ceiling, even though —

I went downstairs to look for Mom. She wasn't there. She wasn't in her bedroom. What a mess there was in her room — a million little piles of scrunched-up Kleenexes that looked like a snowy miniature mountain range. Grandma had gone to bed. I went outside and sat on the second-floor deck stairs and threw clothespins into the pail. I missed every shot. It was dark, which was why. I went inside and slipped the pages of Mom's totally insane and unfinished letter under her bedroom door curtain. Then I opened the curtain and took back the pages and put big red exes on all of them starting from each of the four corners. I slipped them back under her curtain. Then I opened her bedroom-door curtain again and took the pages and wrote on the first one: *When can we meet to discuss your work.* I returned them under the curtain. I went to my bedroom and lay down. I got up and went back to Mom's bedroom and opened the curtain and took the pages and crossed out my question so none of it was visible. I didn't want to talk about her work. I slipped the pages under her curtain. I went to my bedroom and lay down on my bed and turned off the light. I held my hand in front of my face and waited for my eyes to adjust to the darkness so I could see it. Finally I saw it. I got up and went to Mom's bedroom and opened the curtain and took her pages to my bedroom and put them at the back of my closet with my broken toys from when I was a kid.

7.

Early this morning mom went off to have an ultrasound of Gord that we could put on the fridge and Grandma was sitting at her table playing online Scrabble with a person whose code name was SINtillating. I don't want to put a naked picture of Gord on the fridge, I said to Grandma. That's mean and stupid. Grandma said Gord is a fetus in utero, not *naked.* What happens to a kid if everyone in her family is insane? I asked Grandma. Well, for starters, said Grandma, I think quite a bit of anxiety? I nodded. And . . . being scared? said Grandma. I nodded. And sad? Mmmmhmmmm, I said. And angry? said Grandma. Hmmm, I said. Why do you ask? said Grandma. Are you writing a story?

I dropped to the floor to pick up her hearing aid batteries and morning pills.

Come, said Grandma. She leaned over and pulled me up off the floor. She pulled me right into her lap. She rocked me back and forth like a baby. Her arm knocked her other pills off the table and also her computer mouse. They just lay on the floor. She rocked me and rocked me. SINtillating is waiting for you to make a move, I said. I had a hard time saying it. Grandma laughed. I lost this game a long time ago, she said. But it's not good to forfeit, I said. You were the one who said the Raptors had to play hard to the final buzzer! Get your head in the game, Grandma!

All right, she said. She banged her fist on the table. Let's do it!

I got off her lap and picked up the mouse from the floor.

Grandma made a word. SINtillating wrote back on the side of the board in the comments section: *Oh, damn, I thought you'd forfeited.*

Never! wrote Grandma. *Your move.*

Grandma and I waited and waited. Grandma drummed her fingers on the table. I chewed my nails. Finally, SINtillating made a word: *lozenge.* Whoa! said Grandma. Nice one. A bingo with a zed! Grandma moved her arms up and down to worship SINtillating like she'd just made a half-court three at the buzzer. Grandma was on the ropes. She made a word that wasn't a word, using SINtillating's zed. *Blazen.* What is that? I said. Nothing, said Grandma. I'm calling her bluff. It's my only hope.

Grandma and I stared at the screen waiting for SINtillating to accept the word or to challenge. Grandma was smiling. She was really enjoying this bluff. SINtillating started typing something on the side of the board. Oh shit, said Grandma. She's challenging it! Then SINtillating deleted what she was typing. Grandma and I went back to waiting. I was so nervous, but Grandma laughed. SIN-tillating made another word on the board — which meant she'd accepted *blazen*! Grandma and I did our sitting victory dance. In the end Grandma lost the game but she was so happy that she'd got away with *blazen.* I knew she would tell Mom about it the instant Mom walked through the door.

After that, Grandma told me she wanted to get a manicure, a pedicure, a haircut and electrolysis on her chin hair. She was going to take the bus and the streetcar all the way to Scarborough to visit the woman she always sees about this stuff. I like her! said Grandma. It's worth the trip. She does it in her home. Grandma asked me if I wanted to go with her. We could stop along the way and look at the lake and skip stones into it. She would show me how.

You'll have a heart attack! I said. She said no, in all the records of all the causes of heart attacks there has never been any mention of skipping stones. In fact, heart attacks are avoided by skipping stones, she said. And by flossing, I said. If you say so! said Grandma. I looked at the hairs on Grandma's chin. I can pull them out with tweezers, I said. She said no, they'd grow back thicker and darker until she would have a full beard like James Harden. Then she asked me if I knew why she suddenly wanted to get all this stuff done to her. Before I could answer, she said because she's going on a trip!

What do you mean? I asked her. She told me she had made a decision that morning to go to California to see her nephews in Fresno. Does Mom know? I asked. Not yet, said Grandma. Scorched earth, I said. I know it, said Grandma. Which is why I must frame it carefully. And which is why I need you to get my credit card and go into my computer to book me a ticket now before Mom gets home. I don't want to aid and abet you in crime, I said. It's not a crime, said Grandma. It's not a contravention of the criminal code to visit your nephews in

Fresno. If the ticket is booked and paid for then your Mom will have a harder time telling me I shouldn't go. It's now or never, said Grandma. I can still breathe, that's the main thing. And Gord will be here soon and I won't want to go on a trip then. And it's cool enough yet in Fresno that I shan't perish (she said perish like "pedish" to sound like the British ladies in her shows) in the heat. I've already talked to Lou and Ken on the phone and they're really excited about me coming — so teddy not and fitch my red purse!

Grandma slowly opened the lid of her computer with both hands like she was peeking into a coffin. Let's do it, Swiv!

It took a long time. It was confusing and I kept timing out and having to start over. Partway through we heard something at the front door and Grandma said oh Lord, here comes the reckoning! But it was just flyers getting pushed through the slot. Do you agree not to bring explosives onto the plane? I asked Grandma. She said yes, yes, just say yes to everything and click on continue. Well why don't you do it if you know how! I said. Grandma said no, no, that would take forever with her useless hands. When this thing busts open they're gonna find *my* fingerprints all over it! I said. Will you take the fall for me? said Grandma. You're a minor so they'll give you a reduced sentence. I'll visit you every day. Do you want a window or aisle seat? I said. Aisle! said Grandma. When my diuretic kicks in I'll have to make a mighty beeline for the toilet. Peeline, I said. And you should walk around on the plane every thirty minutes so you don't get a blood clot. All righty, Shecky Greene, said Grandma. I'll have to get you to put my compression socks on me, she said. Oh no! I said. Not the compression socks! I put a fake gun to my head and blew my brains out. Are we done? said Grandma. You have to switch planes in San Francisco, I said. Fun and games! said Grandma. She started to sing a song about leaving her heart in San Francisco. Will ninety minutes be enough time to get to the other terminal? I asked her. You can barely walk! Grandma said oh yeah, she'd get someone to push her in a wheelchair. Not a problem, not a problem. I typed in her credit card number and pushed *purchase.* Boom! I said. It's done. Ma'am, you've just won an all-expenses-paid round trip to Fresno, California! Man! said Grandma. We're racking up the W's. Grandma and I did the sitting victory dance *again.* I wanted to ask Grandma how you could leave your heart in some city and then sing about it because you'd obviously be dead.

Mom still wasn't home. Grandma and I memorized some more trucker lingo. *Watch out, Smokey's at your back door.* We had First Aid class. Grandma taught me how to do a fireman's lift. She could carry me and walk around at the same time because of the *weight displacement* of my body across her back. Grandma used to be a nurse. She hated how the doctors bossed around the nurses. The nurses had to connive and connive. They knew way better than the doctors and got paid way less, hardly anything. When Grandma was in nurses' training she had to show her teachers her Kotex to prove she wasn't pregnant because why train a lady to be a nurse if she's just going to go and have a baby? Grandma walked with me on her back to the living room and back to the dining room and then to her bedroom and back to the dining room. When we went through her bedroom doorway my head knocked against it and I said hey, learn how to drive, lady and she had to put me down for a minute. I just have to *hoooooo,* she said. This fireman's lift is if you are in the bush, she said, and the person can't walk. Then she taught me how to make a splint out of things lying around and how to make a tourniquet so a person wouldn't bleed to death and how to deal with someone's tongue so they wouldn't choke on it while they were having a seizure. I asked Grandma what about how to amputate a limb in an emergency situation. Hmmm, said Grandma, I'm stumped. That was her joke. But how? I said. Well, said Grandma. She thought *quickly* was how. Very quickly, and hopefully there would be some hard, hard liquor on hand. I asked Grandma if she knew how to give someone a tracheotomy with a Bic pen. She said she'd heard about that but wasn't it an urban myth or something? The phone rang and it was Shirley from her hometown telling her that Gladys had died. Grandma had the phone on speaker to hear it better and Shirley told her that Gladys was found naked by her daughter-in-law in a pool of blood in her kitchen. She'd gotten up in the middle of the night to go to the bathroom, then had gone to the kitchen for a glass of water and then had fallen and cut her head open on a counter and then had taken off her night-gown to soak up the blood and then had passed out and then had died. That was the theory. Gladys was ninety-seven years old. Then Grandma and Shirley switched to their secret language. When Grandma finally got off the phone she told me it often starts with a fall at that age. What starts with a fall! I said. What do you think? Death! she said. At that age it's very easy to fall and often deadly. Then she said, Well! It's a blessing that Gladys hadn't suffered from a long illness. Gladys had been so annoyed to be that old. The only thing wrong with me is that I'm so durn healthy! she'd tell Grandma on the phone. Then Grandma asked me to run downstairs and get her little suitcase out of the basement and pour her half a schluckz of wine.

Mom came home at last with the naked picture of Gord. She had noodles for us from the Spicy Noodle House and Nutella bombs for dessert. Let's have a look! said Grandma. I didn't want to look. Mom showed us the picture. There was nothing to see but black and grey smudges and swirls. Mom and Grandma were smiling so much. There's Gord! said Mom. She pointed at a grey blob with some white patches on it. Wow! said Grandma. She put her arm around Mom's shoulders. She said, Gord. Our precious Gord. She stared at the blob. Mom was smiling and then crying. She has *mood swings.*

But, so . . . I said.

They couldn't tell! said Mom. We still don't know if Gord is a boy or a girl. See Gord's little leg? It's covering up the sex organs.

Mom! I said. Mom laughed. She hugged me. Then Grandma started laughing too. C'mon, said Mom. She tried to pull me to the kitchen. Let's put Gord on the fridge! No! I said. Use the fireman's lift! said Grandma. Put her on your back!

We ate the noodles and the bombs and then Grandma said she had news, too. Oh no, I thought. Hello apocalypse. Mom looked at Grandma. Yeah? she said. She looked excited about hearing Grandma's news. Grandma's strategy was good. Mom was in a happy mood because of Gord being fine even if we didn't know for sure if Gord had any sex organs — which I think is a good thing not to have in life, and I crossed my fingers for Gord.

Grandma said, Well, first of all her friend Gladys had died that morning and she'd like to raise a toast to Gladys and take a minute to travel with Gladys in our minds to a beautiful place, as travel companions, and to see her there safely and to wish her luck and peace and hug her. Mom and I closed our eyes for a minute. I travelled with Gladys in my mind to a beach in Hawaii which I thought would be beautiful but it was hard not imagining Gladys naked and covered in blood sitting in the plane next to me and then rolling out a bloody towel to lie on in the sand. I tried to imagine a track suit for her like Grandma's. I thought Grandma's strategy was even smarter now. By getting us to travel in our heads with Gladys she was putting the idea of travel into Mom's mind, and the beauty of travel, and also making Mom feel sorry for her because her friend had died. Even though her friend had been mad about still being alive and had wanted to die.

When the minute was up Grandma said, Okay! I thought, Oh! That was fast. Okay, Gladys, good luck and peace forever and bye! I hugged her on the beach. And in other news, said Grandma. I took a big breath and straightened my back. I looked at Mom. She was smiling. She looked friendly and calm. I'm going to California on Friday, said Grandma.

You are? said Mom. Yeah! said Grandma. She pointed at me. Swiv booked me a ticket. I've got an aisle seat.

Don't look at me! I said. She had a gun to my head!

So it's all booked, said Mom. She looked at me but I didn't look at her. Yep, said

Grandma. A *fait accompli.* She bounced her hands on the table. I stared at the photo of The Blob. This is the bullshit you're in for, Gord, get ready.

Eventually, after Mom finished sighing and saying hmmm and shaking her head and blowing her nose six thousand times, she said well, I know you're not asking for my permission or anything but it's a super risky thing to do. Well, said Grandma, not really. Lou and Ken will meet me at their end and there are all sorts of people to help me along the way. There are? said Mom. Oh you know, said Grandma. They see a decrepit old woman like me and they just come a runnin'! They just come *skittering across the floor* fighting over each other to come to my assistance. Who does? said Mom. Young men! said Grandma. They love to flirt with me. Gross! I said. Grandma pretended to act surprised. What do you mean, gross? she said. That's how young men are! I covered my ears. Mom *chortled.* I'll walk up and down the aisle every thirty minutes, don't worry, said Grandma. Yeah, right, said Mom. We were all quiet for a while. Grandma smiled and hummed. Mom thought. I worried. Okay! said Mom, the same way Grandma had said okay! after the minute of travelling in our minds with

136

bleeding, naked Gladys was up. Okay what? asked Grandma. I have an idea, said Mom. You should take Swiv with you.

Mom had finally said something that made sense. I wrote it on my calendar so I would never forget this day.

Swiv's not going to school anyway, said Mom. I *can't* go to school! I said. And you need a travel companion, she said to Grandma. A sidekick, said Grandma. My little Sancho Panza. The pitcher? I said. That's Satchel Paige, said Grandma. I'd travel with *him* in a heartbeat. Swiv, get on the blower and book your ticket next to mine. Where's your little suitcase?

Grandma and I did our victory dance for the third time that day. Let's go to Hollywood! I said. Well, we're going to Fresno, said Grandma. It's the raisin capital of the world. Grandma asked Mom to saw up her latest Dick Francis for the trip. It's called *Dead Heat,* said Grandma, it's on my bed. Mom said she wouldn't saw it up for ethical reasons. She refused to saw up books. What if you had to use some pages from a book to start a fire to stay alive? I said. You can't throw the whole thing into the fire at once. You'd have to saw it up! Mom said she wasn't going to saw up books *or* burn books. But to stay alive! I said. Swiv, said

Grandma, can you do it? I'd do it myself but my hands are crazy right now. I looked at her hands. They were hard and curled up like the doorknocker on the giant door at the library. Mom looked at me. It was *a moral dilemma.* Why isn't it ethical to saw up a book? I asked Mom. Grandma had already gone to her bedroom to get *Dead Heat.* She came back into the kitchen and plunked the book down on the cutting board and took the bread knife out of the drawer. Oh for fuck's sake, said Mom. All right, I'll do it. I'm gonna make a video that I can use to blackmail you about your ethics, I said. I took out my phone. Grandma laughed. She told me to go pack my little suitcase. I don't know why she always calls it a little suitcase because it's just as big as hers. Or should we share one? she asked. There's no room for my stuff with all your drugs, I said. Mom was at the counter sawing away. She told Grandma to stop laughing and to sit down and catch her breath. She was huffing and puffing from walking to and from her bedroom too fast. I googled Fresno. It's right in the middle of California. It has the worst air quality in the entire United States. I told Grandma she might not be able to breathe in Fresno and would die. She said what on *earth* are you talking about! You can barely breathe here, I said, and in Fresno you'll probably die! Well, said Grandma, then it's a good thing you're coming with me. To watch you die? I said. To *keep* me from dying! said Grandma. How the holy hell am I supposed to do that! I said. I don't want to watch you die in Fresno!

Grandma said she heard me. She'd watched many people die in Fresno. What! I said. Grandma started listing all the people she'd watch die in Fresno. My sister Irene, she said, my cousin Liesl. My other cousin, Simple Jake. What were you all doing there? I said. Were you in some kind of army? Grandma said she had a lot of relatives in Fresno because a bunch of people from her town of escaped Russians decided they didn't want to freeze to death in Canada anymore, they wanted to suffocate to death from bad air instead. Listen, said Grandma, have I ever told you about my friend Huey?

Oh here we go, said Mom from the kitchen. She was still sawing *Dead Heat*. Another one of your *friends*. Listen, Swiv, Grandma said. This is what my friend the revolutionary, Huey P. Newton, said. You can only die once so don't die a thousand times worrying about it. I looked at my phone. Isn't that great! said Grandma. I *love* that! Mom said god*damn*it I want to smoke a Marlie so bad right now. Grandma got up from her chair slowly and it looked like she might fall over so I grabbed her. It starts with a fall! I said. What? said Grandma. That's what you said about your friend Gladys. And then poof, you're dead and naked. Grandma laughed. She said I know which one *you'd* rather be, Swiv!

What are you talking about? I said. I don't ever want to be dead or naked!

I know, I know, said Grandma. But if you were dead you wouldn't have to worry about being naked. Or anything, said Mom.

You're *alive* and you don't worry about being naked, I told Grandma. She said that was true. And she wouldn't worry about being naked when she was dead in Fresno either.

Mom gargled oregano oil when she was finished sawing and didn't wipe it off the sink when she spit it out. I had been planning to talk to Mom about her letter-writing assignment but now I was too mad to be professional about it.

8.

Today was thursday and Grandma and I went to Scarborough for her bodywork. Mom helped Grandma shower and wash her hair even though Grandma likes it better when I help her because I'm more gentle, and I did all our laundry for the trip to Fresno and went to Shoppers for Grandma's meds. The pharmacist's name is Zainab and she's a friend of ours now because we're such regulars and she knows everything about Grandma's drugs and always phones to remind her when it's time to renew them. One time she even brought them over to our house and stayed for conchigliettes and told us pharmacy stories about mixing up prescriptions and getting sued and people going nuts and dying and anyway, they're all *confidential.* Today she asked me if Grandma was finally ready for the bubble packs and I said no way, Zainab! Not the bubble packs! Bubble packs mean the end! Zainab said okay, okay, Swiv, I'm joking, I'm joking. Why do you always shout? I told her because Grandma is hard of hearing and Mom is hard of listening so I have to yell all day long. I even yell in my dreams. Zainab understands me. I get you, I get you, she said. She repeats things I say. All day long, she said. In your dreams.

On the way to Scarborough, Mom rode on the bus with us for four blocks and got mad at three men for not letting her or Grandma sit on the bench for old and pregnant people. I had already found another seat for Grandma and Mom didn't really look very pregnant with her giant Inspector Gadget coat on, so how were those men supposed to know? But naturally Mom got mad anyway and said, Excuse me, but these seats aren't meant for you? The men were all deaf or they didn't want to answer her and they just stared at their phones or into space. Mom said she was pregnant and her mother was elderly so could the men give them their seats? One of the guys said congratulations but didn't move. Then Grandma hollered at Mom from the front of the bus and said, Honey, it's fine, Swiv found me a seat! Plus, Mom was getting off in five seconds at the theatre so why would she even want to sit down and then leap up again right away? Mom said okay, but that's not really the point, and then she stopped talking and stood there silently like a normal person, which was such a relief that I almost started crying.

But then no, she couldn't bear to be normal for more than four seconds and she said to the woman standing next to her that this kind of thing *made her mental* and I wanted to tell the woman standing next to her that every kind of thing made Mom mental and do not respond! Grandma didn't hear anything and just sat happily beside me reading one of her *Dead Heat* sections. I noticed a teenager looking at Grandma's sawed up book and the teenager saw me looking at her and then looked away. My family should never be out in the world.

The woman standing next to Mom said, I know, right? I lose my shit. Mom had found a crazy friend! I looked out the window and saw the theatre where Mom rehearses and turned around to look at Mom and beg her with my eyes to get off the bus now, but without saying goodbye to me and without drawing any attention *whatsoever* to the fact that we know each other. Oh! said Mom. My stop! Bye, honey! she said. Don't forget to cross at the lights with Grandma! Which made it sound like I was a stupid little kid who didn't know how to even *live*. When Grandma was the one who was *hell bent for leather* and wanted to jaywalk but was too slow and distracted to dodge the cars properly and would almost get killed every time. Mom pushed herself and Gord through the people standing in the aisle and bent down to give me and Grandma kisses and then had to shout at the bus driver, who was closing the door, Wait, wait, this is my stop! The driver opened the door again and shook his head and Mom said thank you and *bye guys, bye honey* in a loud voice, waving directly at *me* and then finally got off the fucking bus.

Stay safe, Gord, I said in my head. You are in a very dark place. I'll tell Grandma to pray for you because she's part Christian. My face hurt. I tried to drop my shoulders and read *Dead Heat* along with Grandma to take my mind off being the daughter of the world's most unstable person. Then the lady Mom had made friends with was suddenly standing beside me and said in an even louder voice than Mom, Oh man, your mom is *awesome*! She said it so loud that even Grandma heard her and she said, She is indeed! She's my daughter! One of the guys who hadn't given Mom his seat heard it too and said Mom was a crazy bitch. Mom's new friend said, She's not a crazy bitch, you're a crazy bitch. The other two men who wouldn't give up their seats started laughing. Then Mom's new friend said to Grandma, Oh wow! You guys are three generations! Which was like an obvious thing not an oh wow thing. One of the guys said, Suck it, bitch! Grandma said, That we are! Aren't I lucky? Mom's new friend said, Fuck you, you fucking piece of shit! The bus driver looked at everyone in his rear-view mirror and said they had to behave themselves or get off the bus. The lady talked away in her loud voice about wishing she could come home with us and be in our family!

I had to do something. I couldn't slice my head off by slamming the window on it because they were sealed up to keep children safe. I stood up and said, Oh, Grandma, this is our stop, c'mon! Grandma said, What? We're nowhere near Scarborough! I said, I know, but first we had to stop at this other place called . . . I quickly looked out the window . . . For Your Eyes Only. Grandma looked out the window. What do you want with a Gentlemen's club, Swiv? she said. She started laughing with

Mom's new friend. I pulled Grandma up from her seat and stuffed her book section into my backpack. Because it's where we're going, I said. Bye, I said to the lady. I whispered it. Okay! said Grandma. She shrugged. Looks like we've got an interesting itinerary! I pulled Grandma off the bus without saying thank you to the driver. Mom can't stand it when people say thank you to the driver when they get out at their stop, but Grandma thinks it's a decent thing to do. She told Mom that people clap and applaud when Mom does her job of acting so why shouldn't people clap for pilots when they land the plane or say thank you, at least, to a bus driver? Mom said applause seems sarcastic and bizarre, she hates applause even for herself, and Grandma asked her how the audience is supposed to express their gratitude for her performance and Mom said just by sitting there quietly. Mom is really embarrassed by people jumping to their feet and clapping their hands together like fucking idiots. When she hears clapping Mom gets really sad. Grandma said that's because it means the show is over. Mom talked about her hatred of applause in therapy but when the therapist tried to understand what she meant Mom said aaahhh, yeah, you know what? Fuck it, just fuck it. Grandma said thank you to the bus driver and he nodded very slowly. My *pleasure,* he said. Enjoy your day. Grandma wanted to say more about her day but I pulled and pulled on her arm and the driver shut the door and we were finally alone on the sidewalk.

Grandma read the sign more closely and then she stood back and looked at the giant pictures of naked women and started laughing her ass off again because I *of all people* had wanted to get out at a strip club. She had to lean against the building, right against one of the pictures of the naked ladies, to catch her breath. I walked a way down the sidewalk so nobody would see me standing outside For Your Eyes Only and left Grandma there struggling all by herself to live. She finally finished getting her breath back and I said c'mon, Grandma, let's go! I mean it! And then, believe it or not, she posed on the sidewalk in the same position as the naked lady in the picture with her knees bent a bit and her butt poking out and her hands on her boobs. I looked down at the sidewalk for things to kill myself with. There was nothing but globs of spit and cigarette butts and a flyer about the end of the world and then Grandma was beside me and she took my

147

arm, laughing, and said hooooooooooo boy, where to next?

We finally made it to the lady's house in Scarborough. It felt like we were Luath and Bodger in *The Incredible Journey*. Grandma and the lady, whose name is Roxanne, talked and talked while Grandma got her manicure, pedicure, electrolysis and haircut which included *a stacked nape.* We were in Roxanne's basement salon. Roxanne's husband was home from work because he was sick. We heard him stomping around upstairs but we never saw him.

Grandma was so excited about our trip. She told Roxanne all about Lou and Ken and about all the people she'd watched die in Fresno. Roxanne asked her what colour of nail polish she wanted and Grandma said she'd take the *Lady Balls* which was the colour of the tomato sauce we put on our conchigliettes. Roxanne tried to get me to let her put nail polish on me. I said no because I eat my fingernails, and Roxanne said having nail polish might stop me from eating them. I just need to eat them, I told Roxanne. I don't want to get poisoned. Grandma nodded and said yes, I was at that kind of a time in life when I needed to eat my fingernails. I said, Grandma, I've *always* eaten my fingernails. So far, said Grandma, that's true. Roxanne said she understood. She also used to eat her fingernails. She also used to eat dirt when she had a disease called pica. Now she buys special dirt from the health food store that she can eat instead of digging it up in the back yard. It's the texture of it that she really loves. Grandma said, Well, good for you! You have to eat a peck of dirt before you die.

Roxanne rubbed Grandma's legs with cream. She had to work hard to roll up Grandma's track suit pants. Grandma had her feet in a tub of hot water. I could tell she was so happy. She put her head back and closed her eyes. She told Roxanne to look at her twisted roots and Roxanne laughed. She said, Well you're getting old, and Grandma said, I'm not getting old, I *am* old! Roxanne massaged Grandma's feet. Grandma chose the colour *You Couldn't Handle Me Even If I Came With Instructions* for her toes.

Then Grandma had her electrolysis and it was terrible to see. I couldn't watch. Roxanne had a sharp needle she plugged in and then zapped Grandma's chin and upper lip with it. I asked Grandma if it hurt and she said *hardly*! Everything made her laugh. Even if she's not laughing Grandma's head

149

involuntarily bobs up and down. Roxanne had to take a break from zapping for Grandma's head to stop. Roxanne was very patient. She put on music by a band called ABBA while we waited for Grandma. Grandma said she knew that band! I thought she was lying to make Roxanne feel good but then she started singing along to a song called "Chiquitita." She sang in a serious, dramatic way, the way she helps Mom rehearse her lines. The first line of the song was about this girl being tied up with her own sorrow. Grandma sang all the verses, she was getting more and more dramatic with every verse. Then Roxanne started singing with her. She knew the words, too! They both looked at me while they sang like they were trying to tell me something urgent. They sang the final verse which was about being sad, but also about the sun. They were shouting at me!

Finally they stopped. I smiled. I was afraid that if I clapped or said encore they would sing another song that would end with them shouting messages at me. I slowly looked away so that Roxanne would get back to work on Grandma's chin and we could go home. The guy upstairs kept stomping around. Roxanne said he drives her nuts. Roxanne waited for Grandma to catch her breath from singing and for her head to be still and then started zapping her again.

On the streetcar home nothing embarrassing happened except for Grandma asking me if I'd had a bowel movement that day. But she whispered it. She was making progress. There was hardly anybody on the streetcar except for a man who told us an alien had stuck a transmitter into his ass and was tracking him. Grandma said *ouch* and he said he can't feel it anymore but he knows it's there. Then Grandma and the man started talking about the Raptors and the man couldn't believe how much Grandma knew about basketball. She showed off by telling him all sorts of stats. The man said there were some things that were easy to learn about just by watching TV, like the Raptors. And there were other things that were harder, like aliens having to learn about humans by implanting transmitters into their butts. Grandma told the man that was very true, she'd rather learn by watching TV than by putting devices into peoples' rear ends. The man said, Well, true is true, it's like unique, it can't be *very* true or *somewhat* unique. It's just true and it's just unique. Then he said, *You get me?* I said I get you, I get you, like Zainab from the pharmacy. We all fist-bumped. The man

151

sighed really hard after that like he'd just finished all his work for the day.

When we got home Mom was there making dinner and had her music blasting. She was singing along, with the wrong lyrics, to a song called "The Last Day of our Acquaintance." She was in a good mood for some terrifying reason. Maybe because the stage manager at rehearsal had told her she wasn't mad at Mom anymore for calling her illiterate — *which she hadn't but whatever* — and they had a plan to have vegan brunch. Or maybe because me and Grandma were going away to Fresno for ten whole days. Mom told us that Willit Braun had phoned wanting to talk about salvation with her or Grandma and she'd said, Wrong number, this is Satan. She told Willit Braun that she'd heard he'd been shit-talking her and that was *not on,* he'd better *cease and desist* or she would see him in hell by which she meant small claims court on charges of harassment, stalking and intimidation. I could tell Mom thought that was like Olympic-gold-medal clever.

Mom told Grandma her haircut and fingernail and toenails looked beautiful and very SoCal, even though Fresno is in the exact centre of California, and Grandma

152

rubbed her chin and said at least she didn't look like James Harden anymore. Mom laughed too hard at all of Grandma's stories from the day especially the For Your Eyes Only one. Oh man, Swiv, she said, that must have killed you! Then she said, Oh god, I think I'm gonna hurl. She ran to Grandma's bathroom. It was a day of awful sights and sounds.

Hang in there, Gord, I said in my head. Just look your enemy right in the eye and keep moving forward. Sometimes even though Mom is in her *third try, mister!* she still throws up, which she talked to the doctor about and the doctor said it was probably just nerves and Mom was pissed off about that because that's how they dismiss all of what they think of as *women's vague shit* and wanted to get another doctor who would be able to professionally tell Mom she was dying but it's impossible to find another doctor here so Mom just has to live with being nervous and totally fine. Leave the drama on the stage, Mom! I said. Grandma said, Yeah, honey, would it be so bad to find out you were normal? What is this, said Mom, *your guyses little routine*?

Grandma was so tired from being out all day that Mom made her lie down and watch TV for a while before we ate dinner. The usual bloodcurdling screams came from her room. After dinner I packed *my little suitcase* for Fresno and helped Grandma count out all her pills and we all watched the Raptors game together. The doorbell rang once and Grandma woke up from dozing in her chair but she didn't yell *Ball Game.* Mom and me looked at each other like what the hell is wrong with Grandma? I said, Grandma! The doorbell rang! Oh boy! she said. She used her hands to lift her feet off her ottoman empire and put them on the floor and went hoooooo, and then finally she yelled it.

I ran to the door as fast as I could. It was Jay Gatsby. He stepped right into the front entrance and looked around the doorway into the living room and said, Aha! The adults are here, thankfully. Mom and Grandma looked at him. They didn't smile. They didn't get up. They didn't say anything. Then Mom said, Why are you in our house? Grandma said, Or to put it differently, can we help you? Mom got up slowly from the couch, hanging on to her stomach. She looked violent. Listen, said Jay Gatsby, can we talk about this in *a civilized manner*? Grandma started laughing, which turned into coughing, so Mom went over to Grandma and rubbed her back and told me to get Grandma a glass of water. Jay Gatsby was standing there under the swinging lamp in the front entrance. Grandma coughed for a while. There was a white drop of spit on her lips and they were shiny. Mom wiped sweat off Grandma's cheeks with the side of her thumb. Grandma said, Thanks, honey. She put the TV on mute. Are you okay? asked Mom. Just breathe. Grandma said, Oh yes! I'm *absolutely* fine. What about this crackerjack? She pointed at Jay Gatsby. Right, said Mom. She walked to the front entrance and stood between me and Jay Gatsby. Grandma ignored us and fiddled with the remote. She always jabs it at the TV like she's fencing even though I've shown her eighteen thousand times where to point it without jabbing. Jay Gatsby put his hands up like a bank robber. He smiled. How much did those set you back? said Mom. She pointed at his teeth. Jay Gatsby looked confused. Blinded by the light! said Mom.

Grandma turned up the volume on the game to sonic boom level. She hadn't turned her TV off in her bedroom. All the screams from all the rooms were mingling into one cacophonous scream. Mom put her hand on Jay Gatsby's arm. She turned him around to face the door. We are . . . *shinobi,* said Mom. Away you go! said Grandma to Jay Gatsby. She was trying to rescue him from Satan's power. We're not selling our house to you, said Mom. Like, this is where we *live*. It seemed to me like Mom was losing her strength. I took her hand. My daughter is a ninja, said Mom. She sounded tired. So . . . goodbye, fuck off. Mom sat down on the stairs. She rested her arms on Gord and leaned her head against the wall. Jay Gatsby softly closed the door behind him. Guess he got the message! said Grandma. She hadn't heard any of the message. Mom was so exhausted. I sat down beside her on the stairs. Her eyes were closed. I asked her if it was possible to live without a heart, like that somehow you could leave it somewhere and still — technically, no, she said. Not that I know of. Then she said wait, what? What did you say?

We had to fly to Fresno first thing in the morning. Who's Sancho Panza? I asked Grandma. Mom and Grandma argued about us taking a cab, which Mom thought we should do because of Grandma, but Grandma said no, it's too expensive, we can take the streetcar to the UP train. In the end Mom forced Grandma to agree to take a cab by telling her all sorts of crazy things — things that were *just fears* according to

Grandma. *Just shoot your fears right out the window,* she said to Mom.

I set my alarm for twenty minutes earlier than Mom's because I was the only one who knew how to get Grandma's compression socks on, even though there are YouTube videos and Mom could just watch one and focus and learn.

■ ■ ■ ■

PART TWO:
AWAY

■ ■ ■ ■

Part Two

AWAY

9.

This morning I was constipated. Hurry, hurry, Swiv, try to relax, said Mom, the cab'll be here in four minutes. I'm not a shit machine! *She's all bunged up,* honey, said Grandma, it's genetic. God, I know the feeling, said Mom. This pregnancy is really . . . a cigarette and a cup of strong coffee usually helps with that but — Don't smoke! I yelled. They were standing in the hallway outside the bathroom. If there's anything left in the world for Mom to blame on Gord, she'll find it.

Grandma's area of expertise is bowel movements. She walked into the bathroom while I was marooned in there. She handed me a jar of prunes. Have you heard of knocking! I said. I don't have meals on the toilet! I heard Mom telling us the cab was outside waiting, were we coming? That's when I remembered I'd forgotten to put on Grandma's compression socks — and now there was no time! I was sweating on the toilet. I felt like crying. I couldn't be Grandma's travel companion in charge of keeping her alive and be crying all the time. I gave up on my body's *natural ability to flush itself of toxins* and went to Grandma's room to get her socks. She was sitting in her big chair in the living room, all ready to go, staring out the window and smiling into space like she'd just had a lobotomy. She was wearing a white-and-black scarf with birds on it. We're off! she said. She was so happy. No! Your compression socks! I said. Oh god, Swiv, said Mom. She was standing at the door waving at the cab driver. Do that in the cab! Or at the airport!

But I was already doing it. I was kneeling on the floor and Grandma was hunched over me whispering, It's okay, Swiv, you can do it, you're almost there, the cab driver will wait, don't worry. Let's go! said Mom. I was wearing my tight jean jacket and I was drenched in sweat. Don't move! I said to Grandma. Grandma said, Atta girl, Swiv, you got it. My knuckles started bleeding from being caught between Grandma's legs and the compression socks. He's gonna take off! yelled Mom. She really wanted to get rid of me and Grandma. No, no, honey, he's got his meter ticking, don't worry, said

162

Grandma. He's getting out of the car! said Mom. But I was done. The socks were almost as perfect as the ones in the video. Good work! said Grandma. I'm compressed. Let's go!

The cab driver had come to the door and was putting our little suitcases into the trunk. I had our passports and Sudokus and crossword puzzles and Grandma's pills and two bags of gross trail mix and chewable vitamins from Mom and one section of *Dead Heat* in my backpack. I had two other books for Grandma in my little suitcase. They were called *Let Darkness Bury the Dead* and *The Shadow Killer.* They were big but I could saw them up for Grandma when we got to Fresno. Grandma said we'd buy better snacks when we got to the airport.

You can't bring this! I said to Grandma. I handed Mom the CBD oil. Grandma was trying to smuggle it in my backpack. We're going to the United States of Freaking America! I said. Raisin Capital of the World! said Grandma.

One month ago, me and Grandma went to the government store to get cannabis drugs for her because she wanted to try them out. She had to answer a million questions on a form. She circled the same answer for all of them. She didn't know that she was supposed to answer yes every once in a while to get the drugs.

Feeling nervous, anxious or on edge? Not at all.

Little interest or pleasure in doing things? Not at all.

Feeling down, depressed or hopeless? Not at all.

Not being able to stop or control worrying? Not at all.

Worrying too much about different things? Not at all.

Trouble relaxing? Not at all.

Being so restless that it is hard to sit still? Not at all.

Becoming easily annoyed or irritable? Not at all.

Feeling afraid as if something awful might happen?

Not at all.

There was nothing wrong with Grandma! They still gave her the weed. The government knows that old people lie about everything.

I handed Mom the vitamins. Me and Grandma aren't gonna eat your pre-natal vitamins, I said. We're not pregnant! Can you imagine? said Grandma. Mom said vitamins are vitamins. That's so gross! I said. I threw the bag of Gord's vitamins onto the stairs. Mom and Grandma laughed like they were one team of superior people who knew that vitamins were vitamins and I was the other team. Mom tried to comb my hair with her fingers. Don't! I shouted. I like it tangled.

Grandma and Mom hugged and hugged. Then Mom and I hugged and hugged. Remember to wipe the oregano oil off the sink as soon as you've spit it out, I said. Or I'll have to spend fourteen years' hard labour scraping it off when I get home. Mom promised. It's not my life's work! I said. Mom hugged me again and tried to sneak her fingers into my hair. She told me to phone her when we arrived. If we're alive, I said. Grandma was walking down the stairs slowly like a little kid. She put one foot, then the other, onto each stair before moving to the next. She held on to the railing. See you in the funny papers! she said to Mom.

The cab driver fell in love with Grandma instantly and took her arm and helped her down the stairs and along the little path to the curb, like they were a bride and groom. Shotgun! yelled Grandma. She always had to sit in the front of cars. Normal people sit in the backs of cabs, but not Grandma. She wants to see everything and navigate everything and talk with the driver. The cab driver had to move all his stuff off the front seat. He wiped off the crumbs and chucked some garbage into the back seat next to me. A Tim Hortons cup landed on my leg. Sorry, sorry, he said. Grandma got in. Mom waved and waved. Gord, I said in my head, I'll be back in ten days. You can do this. Use your superpowers. Remember there's a fire inside you that you have to keep burning.

So! said Grandma to the cab driver. She looked snazzy in her giant welder's sunglasses. We were driving. Grandma wanted to get to know her new husband. She turned her whole body to look at the cab driver. How are you this fine day! she said. I fired up Beyoncé really fast and didn't hear anything else the whole way to the airport but I saw Grandma and the cab driver laughing in the front seat. I saw Grandma point at me in the back and then the driver looked into his rearview mirror and waved and smiled at me when he should have been keeping his eyes on the road. I took out Beyoncé to be polite and said pardon? I heard him say is it a boy or a girl? I thought he was talking about Gord. My new grandpa already knew everything about our family. The cab driver pointed his thumb at me over his shoulder. She's a girl! said Grandma. She put her arm around the seat to the back where I was and patted the bottom part of my leg like *that's okay, nobody knows what you are, but that's okay.*

At the end of the ride the cab driver and Grandma hugged! Grandma rubbed his arm! He patted her back! They said all sorts of things to each other about hoping the future would be good to them both and then finally, finally Grandma came shuffling after me into the airport. Peoples' stories are so *interesting*! she said. I pulled both our little suitcases and Grandma carried her red purse. We went to the place where they had the wheelchairs. Grandma sat down in a nearby lounge chair and I went to the long row of wheelchairs and picked one out. A man with an airport uniform walked over to me and said I had to wait in a line for the wheelchairs. I couldn't just take one. He pointed at some people standing by a desk. Then Grandma's diuretic kicked in. Gotta go! she said. I went back to the airport guy and asked if I could use one of the wheelchairs to take Grandma to the washroom which was forty miles away. He shook his head. I tried to tell him about Grandma's diuretic, but he kept shaking his head and then he walked away to talk with his airport employee friend about his new transmission which had set him back three G. I took a wheelchair and pushed it over to Grandma. The guy came back and asked me if I had heard what he'd said before. You didn't say anything, I said. You just shook your head. Well, he said, that's a universal sign for no. Grandma laughed. I can think of another universal sign, she said. I helped her into the wheelchair. Put your little suitcase between my legs, said Grandma. And put mine on my lap. I squeezed our suitcases around Grandma in the wheelchair and started to push her to the washroom. The guy said we did not have permission to take the wheelchair. We know! said Grandma. Step on it, Swiv! I really pushed hard. I tried to run. Grandma held on to the suitcases with her arms and legs. Lean into it, kiddo! she said. The guy shouted that we weren't authorized to commandeer a wheelchair. Oh, we know! said Grandma. There it is, Swiv! She was pointing at the washroom. That's men's! I said. Doesn't matter, said Grandma. Let me out! I wanted to keep going to the women's washroom but Grandma was already moving all the suitcases off her and trying to get out of the wheelchair. No, no! I said. Yes, yes! she said. She was laughing. It's crunch time! Then sit back down! I said. She sat back down and put the suit-cases back on her and we went into the men's washroom past confused males washing their hands and right into the giant handicapped stall. The airport guy is gonna follow us in here! I said. Grandma was already sitting on the toilet saying hoooooooooo. No problem! said Grandma. Let him! She was trying to catch her breath. She was peeing and laughing at the same time. I leaned against the wall of the bathroom stall and looked at my phone to give her privacy. I was sweating. This was my first time in a men's washroom. I looked at a text from Mom. It said remember to get Grandma to walk up and down the aisle every half an hour. It said she loved me and missed me already. I texted her that Grandma and I were basically under arrest and we hadn't even gone through security yet. She texted back *lol* and hearts.

Grandma put her hand on my arm. Our adventure has begun! she said. Isn't this *wonderful*? She said it while she was still doing things on the toilet. She asked me if I'd ever seen this thing on her arm. She held up her left elbow. It's the size of a large walnut! she said. She was rubbing it. It was more the size of a golf ball. It doesn't hurt at all, she said. Look, it's perfectly round!

She was really examining it. It's similar to the thing that Shadow had, remember? The vet said it was completely benign. Feel it! she said. No! I said. Why do you have that! Then I was worried that the airport guy would hear us and bust down the door. None of the confused men in the washroom said anything to us even though they could hear by our voices that we were females in their washroom. I'm growing another arm to hug you with, said Grandma. It's part of my personal evolution. I heard a man outside our stall say, Awww, that's adorable. Safe travels, guys! Was he talking to me and Grandma? We could never leave the stall now. We would have to stay until all the current men inside the washroom had left and gone far away from the washroom to their gates and onto their planes. But new ones would come in during that time. How would we escape? I texted Mom: *Grandma forced me into a man's washroom.* Mom texted more hearts and happy faces. Then she texted that she was at rehearsal now but we'd talk later. She loved me *this much.* She sent the wrong emoji which was of a skeleton or maybe she was trying to tell me she loved me to death.

Everything else is a blur in my mind. I tried

to distinguish between the voice of the ego and the actual situation. That's one step in the process of detachment. Mom used to have all the steps written down on a piece of paper taped to her bedroom wall before she tore it down. Somehow Grandma and I got out of the washroom and the men who saw us didn't care except for one old guy who said, My sisters, my sisters when we walked past him. Grandma told me he said that because for him it wasn't right to be in a washroom with strange women and so he had to call us his sisters, and that way, in his mind, we would be family to him. Then at security it took eighty hours to get through with Grandma and all that *rigamarole* which she pronounced like it was Italian pasta with rolling r's. The security woman discovered farmer sausage in Grandma's suitcase and told her she'd have to check it. It was for Lou and Ken. It was their favourite food. They had eaten it nonstop when they were kids in the old town of escaped Russians but they couldn't find it anywhere in Fresno. They'd looked everywhere. The woman told Grandma that sausage couldn't fly internationally. Grandma didn't want to go all the way back to check her bag so she handed over the sausage. The woman said, Oh, nice, when she saw Grandma's nail polish. What is it again, Swiv? asked Grandma. Lady Balls, I said. That's right, said Grandma. I could tell Grandma was super tired already because she handed over the farmer sausage without a fight and said *well, there's your lunch* to the security woman. The woman said she was a vegetarian ever since she'd seen a terrifying documentary about the meat industry but she'd see if her colleague at the other conveyor belt would want it because he ate everything in sight. Grandma said it's good sausage! She'd had to get her friend Wilda to pick it up for her in Kitchener at a black market, so tell him to enjoy it! Oh, he will! said the woman. He's such a carnivore! Grandma said *a man after my own heart*! The woman told Grandma and me to have an awesome time in the raisin capital and to bring home the sunshine. She waved her scanner at us and Grandma saluted her.

I parked Grandma in the wheelchair section of the gate and went to get her a small black coffee and a bran muffin. I felt around in my backpack to make sure all her pills and killers and nitro spray and our passports were still there. I had Mom's assignment in there too, to mark on the plane. Grandma took her *Dead Heat* out of her purse to read while I was getting the stuff. When I came back she was sleeping. I sat beside her and took deep breaths. I worried about being cross-eyed. I tried to force my pupils to the outside edges of my eyeballs. Grandma snorted in her sleep. A teenager snapped his head up from his phone like he'd just heard a boa constrictor hissing in his ear. There was an announcement that people needing help could get on the plane now. I didn't know if that meant us. It felt like it was us. *Dead Heat* fell from Grandma's lap onto the floor. Then a lady from the airline came and told me that it meant us. She picked up Grandma's book and handed it to me. Oh, it's a short one! she said. I told her it was only one section. I was testing her ethics. She didn't care. Grandma woke up instantly like she'd been fake sleeping and did the sitting victory dance. Let's move, Swiv! she said. Load me up! I started piling the suitcases on top of Grandma but the lady from the airline said she would push the wheelchair so my hands would be free to pull the suitcases. Grandma and the lady took off, talking and laughing about being decrepit, and we got on the plane with the other people who needed help. At some point in Grandma's life someone must have threatened to kill her whole family unless she became friends with every single person she met.

Grandma was almost dead and I was completely soaked with sweat by the time I got our little suitcases into the overhead bin and her purse and my backpack and my jean jacket and Grandma's track jacket stuffed under the seat, and then we had to stand up again and move everything around because we were in the wrong seats, and by the time we finally sat down for good Grandma wasn't even laughing anymore, she just sat there with her hands on the arms of the seat going hooooo, hoooooo, looking straight ahead and sometimes sort of but barely smiling at me. Then she closed her eyes and just went hooooooooo, hoooooooo, and the stewardess came over and asked her how she was doing and all she did was nod and smile with her eyes still closed. The stewardess said she'd bring Grandma water. I put my hand on her arm. Grandma stayed the same. I looked at her chest. It was moving. The water came and Grandma didn't drink it right away, just went hooooo, hooooo with her eyes closed. I wondered if I should throw the water at her face. I just sat there holding Grandma's water. Finally Grandma opened her eyes and looked at me and smiled. She took the water. Her hand was shaking. Drops of water fell onto her legs. Na, possup! she said. I took the cup and held it for her to have a sip. Okaaaaay, she said after she'd had a sip. She looked out the window. We had the whole row of seats to ourself. Oh! We're still on *terra firma,* she said. Shall we play magnetic chess?

It was taking a long time to start flying. I'd forgotten the magnetic chess game. The pilot announced over the speaker that we were having mechanical problems. Oh no! I said. Grandma laughed. Can you fish out my book, Swiv? she said. I gave her the section. How can Grandma almost die from not being able to breathe, then be told she's on a plane that's obviously going to crash, and then calmly read her book? She put on her glasses. I took out Mom's assignment to mark. *Freedom comes at a cost.* All the words started to disappear. Everything was blurry. Fucking hell! I got my jean jacket from under the seat in front of me and put it over my head. Grandma kept reading. I was trying hard not to make noises. I accidentally made a noise but I don't think Grandma heard it. Then I felt her arm around me, the arm with the giant walnut on it, the arm she was using to grow another arm. I was so hot. There was snot in my mouth! I couldn't breathe under my jean

175

jacket. I kept it on my head. Grandma held me tight. She whispered to me through my jean jacket. It's okay, Swiv, everything is gonna be fine. It's okay. She kept saying it's okay and holding me. Then she started quietly singing a German song, like a lullaby for babies. It went *du, du, bist mir im herzen, du, du liegst mir im sinn* and on and on. I took my jean jacket off my head. Grandma kissed my forehead. She pushed my hair away from it. It was wet from sweating. She took a Kleenex out of her purse and wiped my nose. I'll do it, I said. I told Grandma I was having a nervous breakdown. Tell me what's on your mind, said Grandma. I told Grandma I was scared she was going to die and that Mom was insane and would kill herself and that Gord would die and Dad would be killed by fascists and never come home and I'd be alone forever, and then Jay Gatsby would take the house from me and then I'd die from hunger or from being killed by cops.

Grandma nodded. She put her *Dead Heat* into her purse. She put her arm around me again. She said, Okay, Swiv, I hear you. She kept nodding her head and made her face tiny. She held me like that with her face all small from thinking until I had stopped crying and was normal again. Then she said she wanted to tell me a story. What's it about? I said. Mom, she said. Mom? I said. Does it have a title? Grandma said, Well, why don't we call it The Truth. The Truth about Mom? I said. Well, said Grandma. Yes, and other things. But mostly about Mom.

We still weren't flying. I took the magazine out of the pocket on the seat in front of me and opened it to an ad that said *Literally in Love with Jumpsuits.* I put it back into the pocket. I looked out the window at the ground. Grandma waited. I pulled the little window blind to close it and then I opened it again. I saw people in orange safety vests zipping around the airplane in carts with suitcases on them. I stopped looking out the window and looked straight ahead. Okay, I said. Tell it.

Chapter One, said Grandma. She looked at me. She smiled.

You don't have to say chapters, I said. Just say it. Okay, said Grandma.

I pushed record on my phone.

10.

So when was it? Let's see. I seem to recall that I'd just returned home from Knipstja's funeral in Rosenort — she was old, so it wasn't unexpected . . . And your mom was waiting for me in the lobby of my apartment block, that one by the river in the shape of a milk carton, with that awful landlord. Momo had died. Yes, she had already died that spring. It was summertime when Knipstja had her funeral. Your mom and I were . . . not ourselves. Of course! We had lost Momo. Oh . . . well, Momo fought so hard. She made all those jokes. Do you remember that one joke? I mean, you were young. Maybe you were too young to remember . . . And your mom and I were in shock. Well not shock, really, we could see this coming but . . . we had all been fighting hard. Momo most of all. But we lost. We lost! Did Momo make a decision to stop fighting? Was it a conscious decision? Well, we don't know. I'd say it was. I'd say it was and we can honour that. We can accept that. Well . . . But the doctors weren't fighting hard. They were clueless. Don't make them deal with mental illness. They don't have a clue. They don't listen! Read Virginia Woolf instead. But I could tell that your mom was . . . what's the word . . . well, just *decimated.* Momo was her . . . I'd say her best friend. I mean they were really in cahoots. We were all . . . not ourselves . . . I mean good grief, Charlie Brown! But there was something else with your mom. This loss was . . . I mean there's loss and then there's loss . . . and this loss . . . it altered something in her. She was full of fear, I think. She was afraid it would happen to her, too. Like a contagion. First your grandpa, then Marijke, then Momo . . . So your mom became very anxious. She became very afraid that she would, well, lose her mind too, and . . . it would happen again. To her.

If you lose your mind can you find your mind again? Of course you can. That's life! So . . . then it seemed as though your mom began a process of . . . well, really of killing herself. I mean, not *killing* herself, no, no, no, Swiv . . . that's not what I'm saying . . . but in a sense killing off her *self,* so that . . .

she *couldn't* kill her physical self. In a sense, ending her life as she knew it. Not ending her actual life, of course, but . . . ending something inside herself in order to protect herself. Does that make sense? And that's about survival.

Hooooooo . . . so where was I? Right, your mom met me in the lobby after Knipstja's funeral. I remember thinking that she was so thin. But she had these skinny jeans. Stovepipes! And she had that cast on her arm! Remember, from falling off her bike that night when it was raining so hard. And she had these red blotches around her eyes. They were different than your Nike swooshes. I hugged her so tightly then, in the lobby . . . I felt her bones. I was afraid I'd break them. We sat down on one of the couches. Those stupid couches that were so soft you couldn't get back up. I knew she was suffering, so deeply sad, so lost and so afraid. She was sad and she was afraid, but she wasn't crazy, Swiv. I shouldn't use that word, *crazy,* I know. She was fighting, fighting. She was fighting on the inside. Sometimes when we fight . . . sometimes we're not fighting in quite the right way . . . we need to adjust our game. But still, the main thing is that we're fighting . . . your mom's a fighter. We're all fighters. We're a family of fighters. What can I say! And then she told me that she had been offered a part in a movie being shot in . . . some corner of Albania! I remember feeling very surprised by that but also thinking, Oh, great! That sounds interesting. Your mom needed to get back into life, back into work . . . it was something to look forward to and to focus on . . . well, I had mixed feelings about it but mostly I thought . . . good! What's the worst thing that can happen? That's what I thought then. Well . . . silly me.

And we talked about it for a long time that day. She talked about how hard it was to get roles now at her age, and being a woman . . . She told me about the movie, although she didn't really know too much about it . . . But it was some European director, you know, and it could be a good break . . . could lead to other work. And she said she'd talked about it with you and your dad and her friends and it seemed to her like it was a good idea . . . She said you and your dad could go and visit her and stay with her there . . . not that they could afford it . . . it was summer so you didn't have school . . . although you and school have always had a . . . tepid relationship. Anyway . . . and she said she'd only be gone for six weeks at the most. Well . . . it didn't turn out quite that way . . . as we know . . . but in the lobby that day she was *excited* about it. Her eyes were . . . they were flashing again! It was just so good to see her excited about something, so I . . . I said good! Do it! It seemed like a good idea. Just . . . to keep working. And to go away for a while. So then . . . she went!

But strange things happened on that set . . . First of all, somebody took that cast off her arm . . . sawed it off . . . and it was too early, her arm hadn't healed but the people there said no, she couldn't have it on her arm in the movie . . . I remember her telling me that on the phone . . . she had somehow managed to get a signal on her phone . . . she was standing on a big hill when she told me that they'd taken the cast off . . . some farmer had taken her into his barn and sawed it off . . . and then later that day in a scene they were filming she had to use that hand, the one the cast had been on, to smack a bunch of mosquitoes on the wall . . . she used, you know, the *heel* of her hand . . . and it was still broken! That was very painful for her . . . very painful . . . But that was nothing in the scheme of things, that was only the beginning . . . It was so hard for me to communicate with her because the crew were off in a remote place . . . I don't even know where, exactly . . . but in the north of Albania . . . It was hard for her to get her phone to work and I could never get through to her . . . even e-mail was touch and go.

Hoooooo, hmmmmm . . . so . . . well . . . that was a problem. Especially for you and your dad. I mean, I believe now that we . . . we *adults* in your life . . . that we didn't pay close enough attention to you during that whole time. We were all so . . . there's a low German word . . . I don't know . . . we were in shock I guess . . . bedudtzt . . . that's the word. That's a good word, isn't it! Goanst bedudtzt. Oba yo. Momo was gone . . . and we didn't stop to think that you had also lost Momo . . . and she loved you so much. She always had such zany ideas . . . do you remember, Swiv? You were always going around with her on the bus to funny places . . . exploring . . . And then, really, you were left to your own devices . . . Your dad, I mean he took care of you when your mom was gone, he made meals and put you to bed and everything else . . . But he was in a fog of his own, and then his drinking was getting worse and worse *by the minute* while your mom was away, and he couldn't reach her and she wasn't calling, and we just didn't know what was really happening.

I remember coming to your place one evening and your dad was there on the back porch all wrapped up in a blanket . . . just staring off into space . . . smoking, smoking . . . always with a drink . . . always ice cubes clinking. His hands were so chapped from the cold because he couldn't hold his cigarettes with mittens on . . . I remember thinking well, good, there are ice cubes in his drink! That will water it down at least. I sat with him and we talked a bit. I don't even know if he was still going in to work . . . and I didn't know where you were. Were you in your room? Or off playing with friends? I should have known where you were . . . I'm sorry, Swiv. I mean, I knew you were *around.* But I should have made it my business to talk with you, to . . . really talk with you! I'm very sorry about that . . . no, no, I know you'd say it wasn't . . . but I'm telling you, okay? That's . . . that's what happened! Hooooooo . . .

And that's how it went for quite a while . . . at the beginning, in the first few weeks, we did hear occasionally from your mom, if she could get the internet . . . it sounded like she was having fun, and there were funny stories . . . the director was a hoot . . . well . . . she was upbeat in her letters. She talked about wanting you and your dad to come visit her there . . . but then . . . she stopped writing as much, and then . . . there was just radio silence. So . . . listen, why don't you put that . . . put your jean jacket here . . . oh, here's a blanket, do you want to curl up in it? We're still on the ground. Look at that! Well, I wonder about this mechanical difficulty . . . enna-way, it happens. Don't worry! It happens all the time.

So . . . well, and then the days went on . . . we all waited for your mom to call or to e-mail. I don't know . . . I don't think your dad was going to work then. You had stopped going to school, too . . . we were in *a holding pattern.* Now, when I think about it, I think I should have gone there, to Albania. I should have got on a plane and gone to your mom . . . What's that? Oh, I know, honey, you're right. Shred the guilt! You've heard me say that so many times, haven't you! It was my friend Wilhemina who said it to me first . . . it's a true thing . . . it's good . . . But . . . yes. Ach, yes. Yo, yo, yo . . . Do you remember my friend Wilhemina? Here, pull that blanket over your knees . . . there we go, sweet-heartchen.

Hoooooooo . . . so . . . that's where we were at! Oh. Yes, please . . . thank you. Swiv, would you like . . . could we get another glass of water, please? Why don't you put your little tray down. It's that little knob . . . yeah . . . So . . . none of us could connect. We couldn't connect with each other, we couldn't connect with your mom. Wilhemina came to my apartment almost every day and we played several games of Scrabble in complete silence. She'd make tea in my kitchen . . . and your dad always on the porch with his drink in his glass, but where were you? Where were you that whole time? What were you thinking? Swiv, I have to apologize to you, again. I'm so, so sorry . . . you must have felt absolutely abandoned! And then all that nonsense from your school . . . *conflict managers* . . . ha! You needed your mom. You needed your dad! You needed me. You needed Momo. You needed someone! I guess that was basically the beginning of your . . . you know . . . sort of fractured relationship with school . . . Well, it stands to reason! You were a fighter. We were . . . blind. You were basically taking care of your dad . . . he had checked out, really, he was frozen . . . you were running the household! I asked your dad if you should come and stay with me but he said no . . . I think he would have just fallen apart entirely if it hadn't been for you. He had the notion that he needed to take care of you, but it was you taking care of him . . . And we . . . hoooooo . . . but okay! So then . . . then what happened? Well . . . exactly. What did happen? Your mom eventually came home. She had been away for four months. And then . . . Well . . . She came home.

And . . . and . . . oh, for Pete's sake . . . I do apologize. Just one second. I think I've got some tissue here . . . Oh, I'm emotional! Well . . . one moment, please. Uno momento. Let's break for a word from our sponsors! Hooooo . . . okay. So. Thanks, honey. So. Your mom came home and she had . . . well, a lot had happened to her over there.

Oh, I mean she was wild-eyed when she came home. Just . . . wild-eyed! We were all frozen, we were all just paralyzed because we didn't know what to do or say. I mean . . . she was so skinny and her face and her arms were tanned, so brown from being outside . . . her face was so thin and bony and brown and then her huge pale, pale eyes like . . . I don't know what. Now I think that she was getting rid of her old self. She was getting rid of the self that was vulnerable, the self that had maybe inherited this horrible disease . . . her *genetic legacy.*

Maybe. Or she was getting rid of what she was afraid would be her fate. I could be wrong . . . but I think she was fighting to be someone else . . . and to live. But in the process she was coming to the edge of death . . . not death but . . . ohhhhh . . . it was hard to watch. Yup, yup, yup, yup, yup . . . She would come to my apartment and sit at my table, that little table in the kitchen . . . and we'd talk. At first not very much. She couldn't sit still for very long. She was going for long, long walks . . . I worried about you. I talked with your dad on the phone. He'd almost given up. He didn't know what to do. He didn't know who she was anymore, he said. She had started taking anti-depressants. She had started taking sleeping pills. She was getting thinner and thinner. She didn't cry, she didn't laugh. She didn't eat. She didn't read. She didn't sleep. She was . . . rigid. Just frozen. I'd call asking where she was, how you were . . .

Then she started talking to me more. She always talked about you. She was so worried about you. She said she had destroyed her family. She said she was a terrible mother. She looked at herself in family photos, that one on the wall in the dining room from that trip to . . . wherever . . .

Paris or what have you . . . and she couldn't recognize herself. She'd sit there and stare at it for hours trying to find herself in it. Then one day she told me about what had happened in Albania.

We're still on the ground, for Pete's sake . . . are you warm? Are you okay, sweetheart? Do you want the rest of my bran muffin? . . . So . . . I remember that day very clearly. The sun was on her hair, on the side of her face. We were sitting at my little kitchen table, which was unusual. Normally we'd sit at the dining room table or in the living room. She was always standing up and pacing, pacing. But this time she sat still at my kitchen table, with the sun on her face . . . She looked beautiful, she looked lit up from the inside. You know that fire inside, Swiv? It was still there. It was burning. I waited for her to talk. We sat looking at each other . . . Then she said, Mom, I did a horrible thing . . . she was so serious . . . I asked her what she'd done and she said she'd had an affair with somebody from the film . . . not the director . . . someone else, I don't know who . . . but when she said this . . . I couldn't help it, but I laughed! I said, Honey, an affair? That's not a *horrible* thing . . . Swiv, sweetheart, you have to understand, the relationship between your mom and your dad was . . . And I wanted to laugh so hard . . . from relief or I don't know what . . . but your mom was crying then . . . and I didn't laugh any more. She said she had destroyed her family, she had destroyed *you.* I held her. I held on to her for so long . . . Well, in my opinion but what do I know . . . it's not a big deal. It happens! It's life! But here's the thing! Swiv, here's the thing! I don't think this was that kind of affair, the kind you have when there's trouble brewing at home. She loved your dad. It was something else. And enna-way the affair was just a by-product. But she didn't see that then. She just felt so guilty . . . she kept saying over and over that she had destroyed everything she loved.

And then she told me this . . . I'll summarize but . . . you know, your mom's letters home didn't really tell what was happening in Albania . . . You know your mom . . . the letters were funny, she was making light of everything . . . but I went back over them later, after that day in the kitchen, and I could *see* what she had been alluding to. She told everything as a funny story in her letters . . . she knew what details to use to make things funny and what details to leave out so I wouldn't worry . . .

or maybe she wasn't even worried, consciously, herself . . . at that time. But . . . when I went back and reread the letters I saw she felt ashamed . . . I saw that she was embarrassed she'd gone to do this movie in the first place . . . The director had asked her over and over, begged her, to be in the movie, and she kept saying no . . . at first. Then at some point, she said okay . . . and she was so embarrassed about that. That she'd let him convince her. That she'd let desperation and vanity and selfishness and grief take over . . . that's how she talked the day she told me the story in my kitchen . . . She said that she shouldn't have left you and your dad to do this movie . . . she was acutely ashamed for having gone . . . so that was part of the reason why she couldn't accept what was happening . . . and why she couldn't change her mind and get out of there, just come home . . . She was saving face . . . and she was minimizing it all in her mind . . . and in her letters . . . and when she just wasn't able to keep minimizing it . . . that's when she stopped writing.

Hooooooooooooo . . . hooooooooooooo . . .

I'll be brief or else I'll have to use my nitro! . . . It's what? It's in your backpack, I know . . . keep it nearby! So your mom just talked and talked that day . . . it was very unusual . . . She had found a tiny window of light in her brain . . . a tiny light, a bit of clarity . . . she'd been looking and looking for that light . . . she was killing herself to find that light . . . she was hunting it down . . . and that day she found it! She just talked and talked. And she told me that she'd been afraid, very afraid, on that film set in Albania. She had thought about leaving, about walking away down the road to Tirana, or somewhere, some town that was still hours away . . . but she couldn't walk there . . . so she thought about maybe hitching a ride from someone to Tirana, to the airport . . . getting on a plane . . . But the director had taken her passport when she'd arrived . . . he'd needed it for some reason . . . he had picked her up at that rinky-dink airport . . . they were, oh I don't know, hours away from anywhere . . . the crew were living in two old abandoned lighthouses near the coast . . . really, there was nothing, nuscht . . . they had to drive for hours from the airport . . .

This director . . . he had pit bulls, these dogs that he'd brought from who knows . . . these fierce dogs that absolutely terrified your mom . . . You know she's already afraid of dogs . . . from when she was a kid . . . has she showed you those scars? Oh, just ask her! Enna-way . . . so it was a small crew and just a few actors . . . Most of them were local so they lived somewhere nearby . . . closer to the town . . . and so the small crew and your mom and the other actor were sharing these lighthouses in the middle of nowhere . . . Okay, so your mom had to figure out these damn dogs. She had to walk from one lighthouse to the other by herself sometimes, at night, total pitch-black darkness . . . just following the moon or stars or what have you, and the dogs, these pit bulls at her heels . . . so she started taking some of her food to throw to the dogs every time she went out of the house . . . to befriend them.

Eventually the dogs became her friends but by that time she wasn't getting enough to eat because she was giving her food to the dogs to keep them from attacking her . . . and there wasn't much food in the first place . . . The director had hired a local woman to cook for them . . . but this woman left at some point . . . people were always coming and going . . . and there were so many fights with the director . . . yelling, screaming . . . all in Albanian or French, which your mom couldn't understand . . . The food was running out . . . somebody was supposed to bring food . . . but the director had to get money sent from some-where first . . . And everything was breaking down . . . the film equipment wasn't work-ing . . . So there was not enough food . . . and not enough blankets at night and it was so cold . . . and not enough clean drinking water . . . The director told them they could all drink from the taps but then every one of them got sick . . . very sick . . . your mom told me she had an accident in her sleep. She shit the bed! Okay, I apologize . . . Swiv . . . it's sickness. It's just the body . . . But it was that bad. And she had to drag all her sheets to the beach . . . and rinse the sheets out in the sea . . . it was the middle of the night . . . and she was so sick . . .

The director got a farmer to give them all pills of some kind . . . But your mom didn't know what the pills were . . . there were many language barriers . . . so she just pretended to take the pills . . . And there she was with no passport, fending off crazy dogs and starving and freezing at night and getting burnt to a crisp during the day . . . standing outside day after day waiting for . . . waiting for what? Waiting for light, for rain . . . waiting for Godot! Most of the time she didn't understand what was being said on the set . . . and the director was always mad, always yelling . . . he was lecturing everyone about preparing to die. They needed to be ready to die! he said. To die for his film, to die for art.

Your mom told me about this young guy from Lithuania . . . this young guy was a grip . . . he'd heard that this great director . . . the director was famous although I'd never heard of him . . . this young guy had heard that this famous director was making a movie in Albania and so he went there . . . He wanted to work for this director. He'd just finished film school . . . but the director didn't want to hire him . . . And the young guy had no money to get back to Lithuania, so he was stuck . . . The director wanted him to sleep outside at first, but then he finally let this guy sleep on the floor in one of the lighthouses. He didn't give him a blanket . . . he didn't give him food. Your mom gave the young guy some food and one of her blankets. She told him to sleep on the couch, not the floor. The director ignored this guy and told him he was an idiot for coming there with no way of getting home. Finally someone driving to Tirana said the young guy could go with him. Your mom wanted to go too . . . she said she'd buy some food or whatnot . . . and come back . . . but the director said no, she was needed for a scene.

After that, your mom asked the director if she could fly with the reels to Paris . . . This would happen every week or two . . . there were so many delays . . . they were waiting for rain, then sun, then rain . . . and someone had to fly back to Paris with the reels every week or two . . . Your mom asked the director if she could do it . . . she thought she could go to Paris on the pretext of delivering the reels and then head directly to the airport . . . and come home . . . but the director said no, she couldn't go because she was needed in the shots . . . And soon after that a bridge was washed out and the road out of town was damaged and impassable . . . or so they said.

And then they shot this one scene . . . yep . . . yep . . . oh boy . . . your mom was supposed to dangle off the side of a cliff . . . and then, well, basically . . . I don't know . . . have some kind of vision . . . or hallucination . . . and then let herself drop into the sea . . . I guess it was an action movie! Enna-way . . . she was terrified to begin with, she was pretty high up . . . I mean your mom is a stage actress, not a stunt person . . . and then something happened with the rope . . . I don't know exactly what . . . some dummheit . . . her body kept slamming against the rock . . . it was really windy . . . nobody could hear her yelling for help . . . everyone else was down on the beach setting up the shot . . . it really was a ways down . . . Your mom told me she started to pray! Please God, please God, please God . . . that sort of thing . . . and telling you how much she loved you, how sorry she was . . . those kinds of last words . . . I mean, she was petrified. And then the director shouted up to her: *Fall!* So she did . . . expecting to drop into the water, as planned, but somehow . . . maybe because of the wind or the . . . who knows . . . she fell, splat! Right onto the beach, onto rocks, onto a pile of seaweed . . . she passed out for a minute or two . . . there was blood on her face, in her eyes . . . I mean, she was okay . . . everyone came running . . . hooooooooo . . . Anyway, she survived, but the director put his head in your mom's lap on the way home from shooting that scene . . . Oh and he cried and cried, he said he was so sorry for almost killing her . . . he cried like a baby in her lap . . .

After that the director wanted her to take her clothes off for a scene but she didn't want to . . . and he was angry . . . He said everyone would leave the set except him and the camera guy and . . . she should take her clothes off . . . it was just a body . . . it was art . . . didn't she understand art? Didn't she understand cinema? Was she such a philistine that she didn't understand cinema? And he complained to the others about her . . . And then she would be left alone in this lighthouse in the middle of nowhere for long, long stretches of time . . . She asked one of the crew if he could get her some books, she needed books . . . but the guy just stared at her. He didn't understand what she was saying . . .

So . . . well . . . there was another guy working on the film who saw all this happening . . . how freaked out your mom was . . . and he brought her food . . . she was still so hungry . . . she continued giving most of her food to the dogs . . . They talked a lot, this guy and your mom . . . and she liked him! He kind of looked out for her. But . . . well . . . then what happened, happened between them. These things happen! She and this fellow formed . . . a bond. The director knew that he couldn't get mad at this guy because he was the best at his job . . . the director needed this guy and . . . well, he needed your mom, too . . . it was far into the shoot and he couldn't re-shoot the whole thing with another woman . . . So he had to accept . . . well, everything.

And then she was supposed to die for good! She had to drown . . . they had an underwater camera . . . there was a riptide and . . . oh, you name it . . . she felt like she was really drowning . . . again, she prayed and imagined you . . . for an atheist she sure did pray a lot on that set . . . and then . . . eventually her so-called dead body was hauled back to the shore and her movie lover . . . I think he was supposed to be a pirate . . . held her body . . . the director showed him how to kiss her . . . they'd put a board on her chest and then draped it with seaweed and rocks so you couldn't see her breathe . . . yeah . . . she died! And then she came back to life. She fought her way back to life. Not in the movie, but in life!

When she came back to us . . . it took her all those months to understand what had happened to her. At first, she was embarrassed. I mean, more than embarrassed . . . She really believed that having the affair . . . which was nothing . . . it was a symptom . . . she believed it had destroyed her family, especially you . . . the person she loves most in the world. The guilt, the *culpability,* was eating her up. It was at that point where one of two things were going to happen. She would disappear right before our eyes. Or she would begin to rebuild. So . . . she started to rebuild! She fought her way back to life. It would take a while but . . . there you are! Here we are. Plain and simple.

But it didn't happen overnight . . . Your mom tried to fix her relationship with your dad. She loved him, definitely, and she felt so awful . . . so awful . . . He would cry . . . that killed her . . . and again she felt it was all her fault . . . He didn't really believe in her depression, or in her taking anti-depressants . . . he was so hurt and angry . . . She told him about the affair . . . and he drank even more than usual. He was turning yellow. His eyeballs were yellow. She checked herself into a psych ward at one point because she felt she was losing her mind, and she couldn't . . . she couldn't stop thinking of herself as a monster, as someone who had destroyed what she loved the most . . . Your dad called her a monster, a terrible mother . . . and then he'd apologize, but he'd say it again, and he'd apologize again . . . she was trying hard, she was really trying hard . . . She hadn't fully understood what had happened to her . . . the fear, the terror, the shame . . . She was rebuilding . . . slowly, slowly . . . and then she found out she was pregnant!

Your mom was happy about that! She told your dad she was pregnant . . . she thought he'd be so happy . . . but . . . he was so mad. He said he knew it wasn't his baby, it was the other guy's baby . . . he kept insisting, and your mom said no, no, it was your dad's baby, she knew it . . . she'd prove it . . . But he wouldn't listen . . . he just would not listen! Maybe he didn't want to know the truth . . . maybe it was an excuse for him to leave . . . Had he wanted to leave? I don't know . . . he couldn't take it anymore. Enna-way, it's *our* baby, Swiv. Your dad left! He's not really fighting fascists. He's just somewhere else . . . and we don't know where he is. Well, maybe he *is* fighting fascists. That would be like him. As you know . . . Swivchen, honey, I'm so sorry . . . I'm so sorry about all of this, but this is what happened, and it is right that you should know the truth. Come here, honey . . . sweetheart . . . my precious Swiv . . . here, let's put your little tray up . . . let's breathe . . . hoooooooo-ooooooo . . .

And then . . . well, and then . . . little by little your mom really did rebuild. She came back to life. She found herself in the photo. She recognized her self. The fire inside. The ember. And here we are. She's not crazy, Swiv. Whatever that is. She might have called herself crazy back then, but she's not now. And she *wasn't* crazy, ever. She was terrified. Her body knew it. It took her mind a while to catch up. She was grieving . . . she was grieving. We're all so clumsy in our grief. She had lost Momo. She was used to Momo fighting alongside her. She had lost her dad. Your Grandpa. And she was so scared that she'd do what they did, too. She didn't want to lose you. In Albania . . . she realized she didn't want to die. She wanted to go home to be with you and your dad. She'd had an affair with that other guy for protection, for kindness — if it was kindness. It was protection. What she was doing was forming a team with that guy. We need teams. That was a good instinct. Survival. She was fighting, fighting, fighting . . . to stay alive. To get back to you. And here we are . . . where's that nitro, honey? Well, that's the truth . . . you know, fighting can be making peace . . . fighting can be going small . . . That's the truth, Ruth!

There was something else that I wanted to say . . . ahhhhh . . . yes! Do you know the story of Romeo and Juliet? Well, I mean in a nutshell. It was a tragedy. Do you know Shakespeare's tragedies? People like to separate his plays into tragedies and comedies. Well, jeepers creepers! Aren't they all one and the same? So, King Lear fails to connect with what's important in life and loses his mind . . . who hasn't? There is comedy in that, don't kid yourself. That's life! And life doesn't necessarily make sense. We're human! Enna-way, everyone knows this. I'd like to see someone . . . maybe it could be you! I'd like to see someone take all of Shakespeare's plays and mix them up into one play . . . bits and pieces to make them one . . . a bit of *King Lear* mixed up with *As You Like It* . . . what? I know, honey. I know. It could be an interesting assignment, that's all I'm saying. Oh, someone did that at the Fringe Festival? If you say so! But I'm saying it should be mainstream, not fringe. To be alive means full body contact with the absurd. Still, we can be happy. Even poor old Sisyphus could figure that much out. And that's saying something. You might say that God is an absurd concept but faith in God's goodness . . . I find joy in that. I find it inspiring.

Oba! I'm rambling. But I brought up *Romeo and Juliet* for a reason. What was it . . . yes! My town . . . my hometown, and your Mom's too. Hooooooooo. And Momo's, of course . . . it had a similar tragedy, in my opinion. The church . . . all those men, all those Willit Brauns . . . prevented us from . . . well no, it was more than that . . .

they took something from us. They *took* it from us. They stole it from us. It was . . . our tragedy! Which is our humanity. We need those things. We need tragedy, which is the need to love and the need . . . not just the need, the imperative, the human imperative . . . to experience joy. To find joy and to create joy. All through the night. The fight night.

That church in our town . . . those Willit Brauns. So smug. So certain. And they caused mass-scale tragedy. They were bandits. They crept in . . . crept in and tiptoed around in the dark . . . we couldn't see what they were doing at the time but we felt it . . . we felt it . . . all those Willit Brauns, they robbed us blind. They stole our souls . . . they hung out their shingles as soul-savers even as they were destroying them . . . they replaced our love, our joy, our emotions, our tragedies . . . rage! Sorrow! Violence! Lust! Desire! Sorry . . . am I embarrassing you, Swiv? Well, they burnt it all down! But listen . . . Our love . . . our resilience! Our madness . . . we go crazy, of course! We lose ourselves. We're human. They took all those things and replaced them with evil and with guilt. Oh. My. God. Guilt! Jeepers creepers! Ah, but we'll slay their hypocrisy with our jokes. High five! They took all the things we need to navigate the world. They took the beautiful things . . . right under our noses . . . crept in like thieves . . . replaced our tolerance with condemnation, our desire with shame, our feelings with sin, our wild joy with discipline, our agency with obedience, our imaginations with rules, every act of joyous rebellion with crushing hatred, our impulses with self-loathing, our empathy with sanctimoniousness, threats, cruelty, our curiosity with isolation, willful ignorance, infantilism, punishment! Our fires with ashes, our love, our *love* with fear and trembling . . . our . . . hoooooooo. Hooooooooooooooo . . . did you find that nitro, honey?

They took our life force. And so we fight to reclaim it . . . we fight and we fight and we fight . . . we fight to love . . . we fight to love ourselves . . . we fight for access to our *feelings* . . . for access to our fires . . . we fight for access to God . . . they stole God from us! We fight for our lives . . . some of us lose the fight . . . oh, it can bring a person to her knees. It can. To think! To think that Willit Braun came around to the house. To think he came around to the house to have us listen to him tell us that Grandpa and Momo are cast out, are unable to enter the gates of heaven. To think of it, Swiv! There are few losses in life that can bring a person to her knees . . . have mercy on our souls. Grandpa and Momo too . . . both of them kneeling on the train tracks . . . All the Willit Brauns, God was the farthest thing from their minds, those scavengers, those thieves, those heretics . . . Grandpa and Momo were closer to God than all of them . . . They knelt . . . they touched death! Finally. Did they pray?

Hoooooooooooooo. Whoa. I'm sorry. A person gets angry. "My tongue will tell the anger of my heart, or else my heart concealing it will break." *Taming of the Shrew.* Do you . . .

Swiv . . . are you awake? Swiv . . . are you awake? Ah! Aha! You got me! Ha! I thought you really had fallen asleep. I thought maybe I'd have to say that all over again! Mamma mia! Whoops . . . Oh look! Look at that. We're moving!

I stopped recording Grandma. I took a big breath and let it out like Grandma does. Hoooooooooo. We were zooming down the runway, then we were going up . . . we were flying! I let Grandma take my hand. I told Grandma, Don't be scared. Grandma laughed. She said she wasn't scared, she just wanted to hold my hand. She said she loved me. And she had the hiccups. We looked out the window at everything getting smaller. Mom was down there, somewhere. I put my face against the little window and said don't worry, don't worry. Don't have wild eyes. Don't worry. Then we were in clouds and then we were in the blue, blue sky. We're in the clear! said Grandma. I'll be back. Her diuretic was kicking in. I heard her talking to everyone on the plane while she shuffled down the aisle to the bathroom. How were we flying? How could such a big heavy thing fly through the air? I heard Grandma laughing even from way in the back of the plane. I took the jean jacket off my head. I could breathe.

11.

I woke up in San Francisco. Grandma was saying honey, honey in a quiet voice. We're here, honey.

In Fresno? I said. I was confused.

In San Fran! said Grandma. She called it San Fran or S.F. or Cisco or Frisco. We're gonna have to hoof it if we want to make our connection. Everybody was standing, waiting to get off the plane. They were all peering down at me in my seat like I was a brand new species they'd just discovered. The flight attendant was calling out numbers and gates. We had to run! The flight attendant made her way through all the people in the aisle and came to talk with us. She said Grandma's wheelchair was waiting for her at the top of the ramp. Could she walk that far? I shook my head. Grandma said, For heaven's sake of course I can. She was pushing through the people in the aisle. She was making jokes. Don Quixote and

Sancho Panza coming through! The flight attendant had already taken our little suitcases from the overhead bin and had brought them to the front. People patted us on our backs and said good luck. Say hi to Lou and Ken! Enjoy the raisins! Grandma had been talking to everyone on the plane while I was sleeping. She raised her hand. Keep on truckin', fellow travellers! she said. Bye, Swiv! said two ladies I'd never seen in my life. Take good care of Grandma! I was afraid they'd say, Good luck with the bowel movement!

Finally we got to the door of the plane. The flight attendant pulled our little suitcases up the ramp and I got behind Grandma and pushed. I thought she was going to fall over backwards on top of me. I really had to lean into it the way Mom takes up the whole sidewalk pushing against buildings for exercise when we're on our walks. Grandma said, Swiv, do you have my red purse? I didn't have her fucking red purse! A man was running behind me waving Grandma's red purse. I've got it! he said. I was still pushing Grandma. He put it around my arm. I said thank you. Grandma was laughing. The man said he'd e-mail Grandma. Yes, do! She was trying to tell him her e-mail address. I've got it, I've got it, he said. She was huffing and puffing. Let's hope we meet in the playoffs, said the man. Well, we'll just see what happens, said Grandma. Trade deadline should be interesting. Playoffs are around the corner, said the man. I've got tickets for game seven against the Nets! said Grandma. You do? I asked. Surprise! said Grandma. Good seats, too. Not the nosebleeders. The man hugged Grandma while I was pushing her. He told me to have fun in Cali. Life is too short for old people to say the full names of places. Grandma was waving over her shoulder, gasping for air. Who is that? I said. No idea, said Grandma. We reached the wheelchair finally and Grandma sat down and I piled our little suitcases on top of her and the flight attendant pointed in the direction of the gate we were supposed to run to. Do you want your spray? I said. No, no, said Grandma. Let's just go! Shake a leg!

I pushed her down a ramp. She sped up and I had to run to hang on. Her red purse strap fell off my shoulder and I took one hand off the wheelchair for a second to put it back onto my shoulder. Then I lost control of the wheelchair and Grandma went shooting off down the ramp. Wow! she was shouting. She said things in her secret language. Na oba heat ex sigh! She was picking up speed. I ran to catch up with her but that stupid red purse strap got tangled around my waist and then Grandma hit a fucking Body Shop stand with her wheelchair. The stand fell over and creams and soap bombs flew everywhere. A man tried to grab the handles on her wheelchair but he missed and she went flying past him. It looked like she might tip over onto two wheels. I was running. I heard Mom calling my cellphone. I knew it was Mom from the ring tone. It was a song called "Fever." Finally Grandma stopped beside a water fountain that was just the right height for a person in a wheelchair to have a drink. Grandma leaned over and had a long drink of water, then she sat there smiling calmly as if this had been her final destination all along.

The Body Shop lady came out of her store and said, What's going on here? I ran over to her and told her my Grandma had hit her stand. I helped her pick up some creams and tubes and shoved them back on the stand. When I finally reached Grandma she looked so happy. She was very proud of herself. What took you so long? she said. I was huffing and puffing. Maybe *you* should use some of my nitro spray! she said. Here, have a drink! She pointed at the water fountain.

I threw her red purse into her lap. Why can't we just do things normally! I said. I didn't know what I meant. Grandma made her face small and I knew she didn't know what I meant either. I sat down on top of Grandma and her purse and cracked the knuckles on both of my hands. I heard "Fever" ringing on my cellphone again. Grandma rubbed my back.

An airport person came up to us and asked us if we needed help. No! I said. Well, said Grandma, we do need to get to our gate quickly. The woman put her pinkies in her mouth and whistled, and a cart that was zooming along slammed on its brakes and stopped right beside us. So far in my life that whistle was the coolest thing I'd ever seen. We piled the suitcases and my backpack and Grandma and her red purse and me onto the cart and took off for our gate. Grandma was still talking. "Fever" was still playing on my cell. I switched it off. Stop talking, Grandma! Just catch your breath! She pretended to obey me. She clamped her mouth shut and opened her eyes wide. She reached out her hand into mid-air and grabbed some pretend breath. Okay, I caught it! she said. She held it in her hand.

I got it right here! I didn't laugh. I thought about how I could learn to whistle like that woman, with her pinkies in the corners of her mouth. I thought if I could just learn to do that I would survive life.

To be honest, telling you all this is making me so tired because I already lived through it and that was tiring enough and Grandma thinks everything is a joke. So just believe me, we finally made it to Fresno. A woman on the plane sitting next to me had a baby on her lap who was one and a half years old. She said the baby was eighteen months old, but I did the math. The woman asked me how old I was and I said around a hundred months. The baby and I had to wave at each other the whole time. I couldn't stop or the baby would look sad and bored and that made me feel guilty. I decided I wasn't ever going to start this bullshit waving business with Gord or we'd never stop. Grandma snored and snored. It took one hour and five minutes of continuous waving and snoring to get to the raisin capital of the world.

Lou and Ken are old hippies! Grandma hadn't told me that her *nephews* are ancient men. One of them was wearing short shorts and knee-high socks with pictures of bulldogs on them. That one turned out to be Lou. He had a ponytail. Ken was wearing jeans and a black t-shirt. He had a white square of hair under his lip the size of one of Grandma's Scrabble tiles. They both had white hair! How could *nephews* be so old? They smiled the way Grandma smiles, as if they think everything is funny and the smiles stay on their faces for a long time and they peer at things closely and keep smiling and seem so amazed at everything.

Wow! said Lou. You're Swiv!!!!! Man! Goddamn! I've been wanting to meet you forever!

Lou and Ken hugged Grandma a long, long time. They hugged me quickly. They were smart and knew things about hugging kids fast which is different from hugging your aunt. Lou did a lot of the talking but Ken talked too. They didn't ask me stupid questions. I liked the sounds of their voices and the way they talked.

Grandma sat in the front of Ken's car with Ken, and I sat in the back with Lou. Grandma was gleaming with happiness. She smacked Ken's dashboard with her giant welding glasses. She did her sitting victory dance. Her head was bobbing away out of control. See the palm trees, Swiv? Obviously! I said. You know these palm trees don't really grow here naturally, said Lou. A lot of them were transported in from elsewhere, you know. Really this is a desert climate, *inat right,* Kenny? That's right, said Ken. And sometimes late at night, said Lou, or in the very early morning hours you can hear them crying . . . they're not happy being here, you know, they're homesick. Yeah, said Ken, you know I've even heard them screaming. That one time . . . remember that, Lou? We were towing John Friesen on his motorcycle. Oh YEAH! said Lou. That tree really was screaming, man. It sure was, said Ken. It sure was. Lou rolled a cigarette with tobacco and papers on his bare knee in the car while it was moving. He rolled it up and put it behind his ear for later because Ken wasn't a big fan of Lou smoking in his car. Lou said one time when Ken's kids were little Lou was sitting in the front seat smoking away and when he was finished he threw the cigarette out the window, but it was so windy and the cigarette got sucked back into the car and flew into the back seat and landed on Ken's youngest son's carseat. Man, said Ken, it wasn't 'til 'bout five, ten minutes later we saw smoke coming off that thing. Luckily, said Lou, the kid was out, man! Slept through the whole thing and didn't ignite.

He *wunt hurt* a bit, said Lou. I threw my soda on him for good measure. Oh yeah, said Ken, he was absolutely fine, didn't even know his chair was burning, but after that Lou stopped smoking in the car. *Inat right,* Lou? Yeah, said Lou, fair enough, fair enough, after that I stopped smoking everywhere, though, cuz I *coont* afford it.

Lou said he'd been working in Silicon Valley and really living the dream, man, Armani suits, collecting art, but then he made a decision to quit his job and travel the world. And right then, in that limbo period between his job and travelling, he had a massive heart attack and almost died, but he had no insurance anymore from work because he'd quit his job and he hadn't gotten around to getting with a new insurance program so he lost everything. Every damn last thing, man! He only had a bike — not even with ten speeds — only one speed and no brakes, and flip-flops and a subscription to *The Nation.* He showed me his heart operation scar, which was a zipper just like Grandma's.

Lou also told me that the Bulldogs were the Fresno State football team and that members of a gang in Fresno also called themselves the Bulldogs. Are you in that gang? I asked him. I pointed at his bulldog socks. No, he said, he just found these socks at an estate sale and really liked them. Then Ken said he had a friend who had once been in that gang and had tattooed a bulldog on his shaved head. It was frightening, man! I mean, yeah, it was effective, you know? Wouldn't you say, Lou? It really was, man, said Lou. I mean he was a friend, you know what I'm saying? I remember him telling me about his dreams. Crazy dreams, man, orgies and . . . naked women, naked men, I mean literally hundreds of naked people all —

Then Ken said, Yeah but further to your point of the Bulldogs, this guy, this friend of ours, quit the gang eventually . . . you know, he got married, had a couple of kids, a straight job. His hair grew all over that bulldog, said Lou. Yeah, said Ken . . . you couldn't see the tattoo anymore so — he became less terrifying, said Lou. Yeah, said Ken. I mean he was a teddy bear. I mean he was doing anti-gang outreach work then. He was a mentor, man. But then you know what? He got older, he started losing his hair . . . see, like mine? And that damn tattoo became visible again, said Lou. Was he scary again? I said. Nah, said Lou, by then there *wunt nothing* scary about him. But his former associates from the gang started seeing that tattoo and remembering things about this guy, our friend, some of the stuff he'd done and how he'd left the gang and you know, they were kind of miffed about that. And the rival gangs, too, they recognized him and wanted to, you know, man, settle scores and the cops . . . well, the cops, said Ken. There'd been some outstanding charges and, well, some misunderstandings . . . so long story short our friend was concerned about his head, man, about this tattoo reappearing. Could he wear a wig? I asked. Yeah, he did do that for a while, but by then, you know, the cat was outta the bag and he was getting scared . . . he was getting scared for his wife and kids too, even his mom, man, and she was one tough lady. She was a warrior, man, said Lou. Everyone he knew was a target, said Ken. So one day he just packed them all up and left town. Took everyone, his wife and kids and his sister and her husband and their kids, his mom . . . just disappeared.

Where did they go? I said.

Who knows, man! said Lou. They just left. Here today, gone tomorrow. Hit the road, Jack. Vamoosed! Ken nodded his head in the front seat. That's right, he said. I miss that guy.

But then if you're friends with him aren't

the Bulldogs going to come and murder you, too? I said.

Lou said nah, he *dint think* so. He smiled. Ken smiled in the rear-view mirror, too. Nah, he said, we're small potatoes. Small fry. Lou said they weren't even potatoes. We're on nobody's radar, he said. Then he laughed and laughed and Ken started laughing too.

Grandma didn't hear any of the story, really. She just sat there looking into the distance and vibrating with joy and wonder the whole time like she'd never been in a car before. When Lou and Ken started to laugh she started laughing too, even though she hadn't heard what they'd said. I didn't want to ruin her happiness by telling her that now we were at risk of being murdered by the Bulldogs probably even before suffocating from bad air quality. Then I remembered that she wouldn't worry about being murdered or suffocating and had seen a million people die in Fresno already, so what was the point. While they were laughing my cell rang. It was Mom. The truth is, it's always Mom. Nobody else calls me on my cell except Gretchen one time accidentally, because none of our parents give us enough minutes.

It took me a long time to get my cellphone

out of my backpack. "Fever" was playing loudly and Lou and Ken started singing along. Oh yeah! said Lou. Peggy Lee, man! Remember that record, Kenny? I sure do, yelled Ken. Why was Lou singing in a sexy way? Ken was laughing harder. Grandma was deaf and blissed out. I found my phone finally but I couldn't hear Mom because Lou and Ken were laughing and singing too loudly and then I heard Mom start laughing, too. Sounds like you made it, Swiv! She started to sing "Fever." Okay! she yelled. This is expensive roaming time! I just wanted to make sure you'd made it! Give those guys a big hug from me! I love you! Make Grandma rest! She hung up.

I'd made "Fever" Mom's ring tone because the song was about getting the flu from being too close to someone. I thought it was a good choice because she holds me tight and kisses me all the time and she's always blowing her nose on me and it makes me sick and gives me fever — but now I wasn't sure it was the right ring tone after all. I didn't want to have a sexy ring tone for Mom on my cellphone! Lou and Ken were still singing along. Grandma's head was bobbing. Lou was dancing in a sexy way. He was moving his shoulders around and around like wheels. Ken was making sounds like mmmmm mmmmmm. Righteous, man! said Lou. I love that Mooshie has "Fever" for her ring. Who the hell is Mooshie? I thought. I said yeah. I smiled. I forced my lips to keep smiling.

Believe it or not we ended up getting to Ken's house alive. There was a woman in it making sandwiches for us. Ken told us she was his lady friend. Her name was Jude. She didn't live in the same house as Ken. She would show us her house later. Ken was helping her do work on it.

Grandma hugged Jude for a long time and said she'd heard so much about her. Jude grabbed Grandma's hand. Oh, what's that called? said Jude. Swiv? said Grandma. Lady Balls, I said. Oh, I love it! said Jude. Jude hugged me too. She said she *adored* my jean jacket and was so excited that Grandma and I were there visiting. What's written on your jeans? she asked me. *Freewheelin',* I told her. I said it quietly. Oh, yeah! she said. She liked that. She told Ken to look at it. She said, Look at this, hon! Ken came over and crouched down and looked at my jeans and smiled and nodded. That's awesome, he said. That's really good. He stood up and said freeeeeeeeeee wheelin'! as he walked back to the kitchen.

He asked us if we wanted a beer. Then Jude held my hand and looked at me and said I had eyes like Ken! Does he have Nike swooshes? I asked. She peered closer at my face. He does! she said. You both do! I love it! Don't you love genetics? I nodded.

Ken showed me and Grandma the room we'd sleep in. It had a bathroom attached to it! There was a large painting of a Chinese man. That's whatshisname, said Grandma. She pointed at the painting. Mao, said Ken. Grandma said, What? Ken said Mao. Grandma kept saying What? Finally Ken and I shouted Mao! Grandma, it's Mao! I said. Whoever he is. Okaaaaay, I hear you! said Grandma. Fun and games! Ken thought that was funny in relation to Mao. Ken told me that Grandma was always hard of hearing, even when he was a kid.

Lou became more quiet when we ate lunch. He was suffering. That's what Grandma said. That's why we came to California. Ken asked him questions. Int that right, Lou? he'd say. He didn't want Lou to suffer. Grandma sat beside Lou on one side of the table. She put her arm around his shoulder. He smiled at her. He said, I missed you, Auntie Elvira. Grandma kissed him. She held his old face between her hands and kissed him. Lou put his arms around Grandma and then he put his head on her shoulder and they stayed like that until Ken said we could all go sailing later.

Then Lou let go of Grandma. He had a tear on his cheek. She kept her arm around his shoulders. Her cup was shaking when she lifted it up for a sip of coffee. You didn't shake like that the last time I saw you, said Lou. I know! said Grandma. Isn't it just ridiculous? Look! She tried holding her cup on the saucer in mid-air. The cup shook and slid all around the saucer. Get a load of that! said Grandma. She laughed. Watch out, Grandma! I said. Lou said he shook sometimes too. I hoped we wouldn't watch him die in Fresno.

Grandma and Lou sat close together. Lou asked Grandma if she'd ever in all her life lost her faith. Grandma said, Oh! Uppy! That's Lou's nickname from when he was a baby and always wanted to be picked up. Of course I have! Yeah? said Lou. *Wunt* you tell us all about that?

She had a fight with God for ten years. That's how you know she loves him. Grandma held Lou's hand while she told us about her fight. She believes that God is love and that love is in each one of us even if we don't believe in God. I've never felt *forsaken,* she said. But for about ten years she stopped praying. She had prayed and prayed that Grandpa would get healthy and be okay. He wasn't. He only got worse and worse. So she stopped praying for that and started praying and praying that she'd have the strength to take care of him. Well, finally, she stopped praying altogether. When her friends and family from her town would ask her to pray for them she would be quiet and try to change the subject because she couldn't pray anymore. But still! said Grandma. She didn't feel *forsaken.* She'd never felt forsaken, even when she was sixteen and desperately sad and lonely and her mother had died and her brothers had put her far away in boarding school and stolen her inheritance. She knelt by her bed every night and prayed, Please God, don't forsake me, please God, don't forsake me. And she felt peace inside herself somewhere. She knew it was there, peace from God, she just didn't know exactly where. Like her will and important papers. She knows they're somewhere in the house, but where? She laughed, and Lou nodded, and Ken and Jude nodded, too. I wondered where the peace was. I wondered what forsaken meant.

Enna-way, Grandma said. That was then. I stopped praying for ten years. Now I'm praying again. When she moved in with me and Mom she started to pray again. That made Lou and Ken laugh. Jude stayed serious, listening and nodding. Grandma said she prayed and prayed that God would make her a good and useful member of our household. Jude said she thought God had really answered that prayer, huh Swiv? I agreed with Jude but it was too embarrassing to say that out loud. I nodded. Grandma winked at me. She kept talking. She said she can't really read the Bible anymore because when she reads it she only hears authoritarian old men's voices. But she knows so much of it by heart and repeats to herself the verses that mean the most to her all the time. And before she goes to sleep every night she sings a song from her old town called a hymn which her mother sang to her, and it's so comforting, and she's always asleep before she can finish singing the song. Do you know the song, Swiv? asked Lou. I said yeah, Grandma sings it to me too sometimes. Grandma said that every night before she goes to bed she also quotes a verse from Lamentations. She recited it for us: *The steadfast love of the Lord never ceases, his mercies never come to an end; they are new every morning; great is your faithfulness.* She cried a bit telling us these things. She made me get her red purse. She fished around in there and took out an old piece of paper and showed it to everyone. It was a note from Mom from when Mom was seventeen years old. It was something encouraging about God's love. Grandma takes it with her everywhere. I decided to write a note like that to Mom too, but I didn't know anything about God. I could write something hopeful from Beyoncé, though, and Mom could carry it around forever. Lou had his arm around Grandma's shoulders. Jude brought her water with ice. Ken had an ice machine in his fridge. Should we sing that song? said Lou. His mom Irene, Grandma's sister, had sung it to him and Ken too! They knew the words. Then they all started singing, half in English and half in Grandma's secret language. Jude didn't know the song. She smiled at them while they sang. She cried a bit too. Lou looked happy. He really sang the song properly and seriously.

I knew the words but I didn't want to sing. I wanted to go sailing. Grandma has good instincts. She saw me dying there at the table with crying, singing, suffering adults and she came to my rescue. Fohdich metten zigh! That's a thing she says to energize herself. She smacked the table. That meant enough of being forsaken or not being forsaken, let's move the blazes on! She asked Lou about starting a marching band. He didn't know what she was talking about, but Grandma said she was dead sure he'd sent her an e-mail a few months ago saying he was thinking about starting a marching band. Then Ken and Jude started talking about marching bands too and they were all laughing and yelling which made me feel like I could leave the table and wander around the house looking at things.

After lunch Grandma and I lay down in the bed next to Mao. Oh! I said. Compression socks! I got up and took off Grandma's socks. It was so easy, they just slid off like straw wrappers. Ah, merci beaucoup, said Grandma. Can you fish out my *Dead Heat*? I got her book and gave it to her. I rolled her socks into a ball and put them in the side pocket of her little suitcase. I went back into the kitchen to get a glass of water for her to swallow her pills. Her metoprolol fell onto the floor. Bombs away, Swiv! she said. I dropped down onto my knees fast and crawled around looking for it. I saw something under the bed. It was a thong! Which is panties. Grandma's metoprolol was sitting right next to them. They were touching. I picked up the metoprolol and handed it to Grandma. There's something under there, I said, very quietly. What? said Grandma. I went to the bathroom that was attached to the bedroom and turned on all the taps and flushed the toilet so Lou and Ken and Jude wouldn't hear me. Then I ran back to Grandma and said it louder. Your metoprolol was beside a pair of panties, I told Grandma. Under the bed. Those must be Judith's! she said. She laughed. Shhhhhhh, Grandma, I said. I got up and ran to the bathroom and turned off all the taps and lay back down beside Grandma. So Jude is Judith.

Grandma took her glasses off and said hoooooooo, it's good to be here. *Dead Heat* rested on her chest like a little tent. She felt around for my hand and I kept moving it over just one inch at a time until she finally got it. That was a game. I didn't want to play it but Grandma loved it so much. Two seconds after she grabbed my hand she was snoring. I watched her book move up and down on her chest. I waited and waited for it to slide off. Grandma stopped breathing. I nudged her with my elbow to get her breathing again. The book stayed on her chest. Then KABOOM!!!!!!!! she snorted, which was how she detonated herself back to life. I was nervous that Ken and Jude would worry there was an earthquake starting which is what happens in California. Grandma stayed sleeping. Her book slipped off her chest but I was ready to catch it. I put it back on her chest and waited for it to slip off again. I couldn't let it touch the bed. That was the rule. I had to catch it ten times in a row before it could touch the bed.

Believe it or not, I know you're not fighting fascism. Grandma told me. It's okay. Grandma told me the word fascism might have the same root as the word for body, but fascism is not the same thing as necrotizing fasciitis which is flesh-eating disease. Grandma said that flesh-eating disease could be an *apt metaphor,* though. Her hospital roommate had it one time and Grandma didn't even care. They traded breakfast trays even though it was against the rules. Grandma wasn't supposed to have bacon even though it's her favourite food and the flesh-eating person really wanted Grandma's yogurt and Grandma would rather chew on broken glass or poke sharp sticks into her eyes than eat yogurt, so they traded breakfast trays and everything was fine. They didn't get caught. Grandma had to have her rib cage sawed open, and then they took her heart out and put it on a bedside table next to her and inserted small balloons into her arteries which they blew up to help her blood flow. They cut a vein out of her leg and attached it to her heart instead. After that they made her walk around to test it out and she didn't even care that her hospital gown was open at the back. Even though there were also men in the hospital. Fighting means different things for different people. You'll know for yourself what to fight. Grandma told me fighting can be making peace. She said sometimes we move forward by looking back and sometimes the onward can be knowing when to stop. Well, anyway, you know Grandma! We all have fires inside us, even you. Grandma said you pour so much alcohol on the fire inside you that it's guaranteed never to go out.

12.

After Grandma's nap we went on Ken's sailboat, which is called *Irene* after his mom, who was Grandma's sister. We drove out to a lake. It's not the Pacific Ocean. Ken said on a clear day we could see the Hollywood sign from the lake, but Jude said it wasn't true. It took three weeks to get Grandma onto the boat because every time she tried to step off the dock into the boat it would move a bit in the water, and then she'd lose her balance and step back onto the dock and laugh for six hours. Finally we were in the boat. Ken made me and Grandma wear orange life jackets. Grandma accidentally tried to get the child-size life jacket over her head and it got stuck halfway down her face. I was afraid the boat would tip from her laughing and shaking so much and from Ken standing up to pry the life jacket off her face.

Lou poured everyone a glass of white wine

to toast to family. He looked sad and happy at the same time. That's a popular adult look because adults are busy and have to do everything at once, even feel things. Grandma put her head back so the sun shone on her face. She looked at her old nephews and at me and Jude and raised her glass up. She said it was good to be alive. She was sitting at the tip of the sailboat and Ken had to keep telling her to hang on to the *gunwales.* Then Lou went over and sat beside her so she wouldn't fall out. She told Lou about how she'd fallen off a banana boat in Jamaica and had to be towed back into shore by six fishermen. Catch of the day! said Lou. Jude trailed her hand in the water and splashed Ken. He smiled and didn't wipe the water off his sunglasses. He just let the drops stay there on his lenses. He looks very commanding, doesn't he, said Jude. I nodded. O captain, my captain, she said. She put her hand on his thigh. He didn't move it away.

Lou and Grandma held hands again. I had a sip of my wine. I didn't want to drink wine. It was so hot. Grandma was turning pink. She was wearing Ken's cut-off UCLA sweatpants because she forgot to pack shorts. She was talking so much. She had to talk loudly in the wind so Lou could hear her. Lou smiled and smiled and hung on to her. I felt the outside of my backpack to see if Grandma's nitro spray was in it. I was sitting next to Jude. I didn't want to think about her thong. I wanted to tell Grandma to stop talking and just breathe but I didn't want Lou and Ken and Jude to think I was bossy. I tried to let my wine slosh over the side of the boat without them noticing. What if everyone on the boat got drunk? How would we get back to the dock? I watched Ken closely to see what he was doing so I could sail the boat if everyone died suddenly from alcohol poisoning. I had my phone. I could call Mom and tell her to call someone American to rescue us. It was good that we were in a lake and not the ocean so we could stay alive by drinking the water and not go insane.

Grandma waved at me. She didn't know she was on the voyage of the *Dawn Treader.* She kept drinking! Everyone kept drinking, and Jude kept splashing Ken and touching his thigh and Ken kept not doing anything about it, just smiling, and Grandma kept talking and Lou kept making sure she didn't fall over the side. Lou looked at me. I liked the way he smiled with half his mouth. I liked the way he hunched over when he sat. He lifted his glass. Jude lifted her glass.

Grandma waved again. She held up her glass. Jude gave Ken his glass so he could hold it up too. Everyone was holding up their glasses. I didn't want everyone to see that my glass was empty from throwing my wine overboard. Would they think I'd drunk it all and give me more? I held up my glass with both my hands around it like a baby so people couldn't see inside it.

Ken took his sunglasses off and closed his eyes. Why was he closing his eyes! He had a boat to sail! There were two more bottles of wine in Ken's cooler! Grandma was still saying things to Lou. Lou waved at me to tell me I should come over there. I walked slowly, all crouched over and weaving, to where Grandma and Ken were sitting at the tip. Her diuretic's kicked in! said Lou. I timed it badly! yelled Grandma. I forgot about the time change! Jesus Christ, I said. I said it quietly like a person in the movies who's all alone in a farmhouse with aliens landing, like Mel Gibson. California is supposed to be relaxing. If you two were to each hold on to an arm of mine I could sit on the edge of the boat and pee into the lake! said Grandma. No! I said. Ken and Jude looked at me. Now they could see I was bossy. I prayed that everyone would be too drunk to remember this day but not so drunk they would die. Lou said there was a motor on the boat. He said he'd take down the sail and we could speed back to the dock. Hang on tight, man, he said to Grandma, and I held her tight too. Lou didn't know about the arthritis in her hands.

Maybe you should tie me to the mast! Grandma shouted. Like my friend Odysseus! She winked at me. She was still drinking! If we tied Grandma to the mast and we tipped, she'd drown. I could hear Mom's voice in my head saying, Why the hell did you tie Grandma to the fucking mast!

Everybody was laughing. Seagulls were screeching away and Lou and Ken were moving around on the boat doing things. Jude stood up in the middle of the boat to take a picture of me and Grandma. To send to Mooshie! she yelled. Smile, Swiv! If I didn't smile for the picture Mom would think I was sad and dying.

Lou loved everything that was happening, even though he was supposed to be suffering. He got the sail down and sat beside us and rolled a cigarette in the wind without letting any of the tobacco fly away and put it behind his ear. He squeezed Grandma's shoulder. He had a thread tied around his wrist. His eyes were exactly the same colour as the sparkling lake. Beautiful, man, he said. Beautiful day. I'm so glad you guys made it out here, man, he said. I hope Mooshie can come out too someday. With Gord! We'd told him about Gord. Gord, man! he said. Grandma hugged him again. She was in love with her nephew! Maybe that was okay because he was also very old.

We zoomed back to the dock. Jude squeezed in between Lou and Grandma. Now she wanted *her* turn to hold Grandma. Everybody loves to hang on to Grandma. Just before we got to the dock, Lou looked at me. He pointed at something far off behind me. Wow, look at that, he said. I turned around to look. Maybe it was the Hollywood sign. I couldn't see anything. When I turned back, Lou was gone! He'd jumped overboard! He was splashing around in the lake making loud screeching sounds like the seagulls. He went under the water and then shot up high into the air and all his hair sprayed water everywhere while he screamed. Jude took his picture. Ken laughed. He's always doing that, man. Scared the everloving shit out of me the first time! Lou swam back to the dock. He climbed up a swaying ladder. His long hair stuck to his face and neck and shirt. What about your cigarettes! I said. Oh fuck, man! he said. And my Zippo! It's an *antique*!

Ken and Jude helped Grandma back on to the dock. Ken pushed and Jude pulled. Now that's teamwork! said Grandma. Hooooooooo. She stood on the dock nodding and smiling and breathing. Then she asked Jude, Now where do you put MAScara again? Jude said, On your eyelashes. That's right, said Grandma. That's right! It was a crossword puzzle clue she'd been trying to figure out. Why wouldn't she stop talking! She and Jude and Ken walked towards the parking lot where there was a washroom. Lou tied up the boat and put the life jackets in a box under the seat and closed the cooler with all the wine and lifted it out of the boat. I stayed with him. I heard Ken and Jude and Grandma talking while they walked away. Grandma was saying she should have jumped in the lake like Lou and peed while she was at it. She said she was very sorry for cutting everybody's boating trip short. She could barely talk. She said she . . . Was. Very. Sorry . . . for . . . cutting ever . . . y's boa . . . ting trip . . . short.

Grandma had saved everyone from alcohol poisoning death. I would have somehow lived but with *survivor's guilt*. I imagined Mom meeting me at the airport and saying, What the fuck gives, Swiv, where's

Grandma? Meanwhile, Ken and Jude were saying to Grandma, No, no, no, it was long enough. We could do it again tomorrow!

Lou announced he'd walk all the way home because he was soaking wet and didn't want to get Ken's car wet. Jude said well if he hadn't jumped into the lake. Lou smiled. It was worth it, man! he said. But you lost your Zippo! I said. I know! he said. He pretended to cry. Then he stopped. He had more Zippo lighters at home. He's got a lot of stuff at home, Ken said. It was only five miles to Lou's house. Ken said he didn't care if Lou got his car wet. Lou said nah, he wanted to walk. He'd stop off at his buddy's place for a beer and a smoke along the way. He'd dry off in the hot air.

I wanted to walk with Lou and not be tortured watching Grandma trying to breathe, but Ken said, Okay man, catch you later bro! Lou put his hair in a ponytail he tied up with his wet shirt. He was wearing flip-flops. Yo Louie, your rosy parker is visible for all the world to see! said Ken. Lou said *eat your heart out, cat.* Grandma said she wanted to visit Lou later in the evening. He put his head in the car window where Grandma was sitting and said he'd really love that, man. He put his fist in the car to bump but Grandma grabbed it and kissed it. He laughed. He told Grandma he loved her. She loved him too. She said I love you too, Louie, so much, sooooooo much. Oh *boy,* do I love you boys! Judith, I love you, too!

Grandma had taken care of Lou when he was a baby and she was thirteen years old. He was as *smart as a whip.* She had carried him and carried him when he cried. Why was Lou suffering? He looked naked when he walked away. His hair was piled on top of his head. He only had his shorts and flip-flops on. He had a cool way of walking down the road and nodding at people in their cars. Lou does his thing! said Grandma. Lou does his thing, said Ken. I wondered, What is Lou's thing? I wanted it to be my thing too.

On the way back to Ken's place, Grandma told Ken that she wanted to get a hole drilled into her head but De Sica had said she was too old. No way, man! said Ken. You're not old! Then Grandma argued with Ken about being old. I am old! No way! I am! You're old too, Kenny! I am not!

Speaking of heads, said Ken. He asked Grandma about the time she had *a bounty on her head.* Remember that? he said. That was crazy, man! Grandma laughed. Oh yeah, that, she said. She waved her hand around like *whatever.*

What do you mean you had a bounty on your head, I said. Oh, said Grandma, just *that*! It was a bounty on my head, you know. Why! I said. Ken said, Yeah, why? He'd forgotten the details. Grandma made her face small to think. Well, she said, I had quite aggressively advised one of my clients to leave her husband, and to take her daughters with her, and the husband objected to this, also quite aggressively. Ken laughed. Quite! he said. Ken and Grandma laughed *pleasantly* together in the front seat like they were talking about splitting a milkshake or something and not recounting a time Grandma was being fucking hunted!

At Ken's place Grandma went to lie down. I knew she was feeling dizzy because she took my arm when we walked from the car to the house and pretended it was just because she loved me. Ken and Jude stood in the front entrance talking with us but I was slowly nudging Grandma towards the bedroom so she could lie down. Grandma said, Okaaaaay. She couldn't really hear what Ken and Jude were saying. Her batteries had died. They were asking her questions but she was saying okaaaaaay, okaaaaaay. She was being polite but also dying. Finally she let me walk with her to the bedroom and she lay down. She went hooooooooooo. She smiled at me. I frowned at her. I felt her forehead. It was cold but sweaty. Wasn't that fun? she said. Don't talk, Grandma! I said. I ran to get a glass of water from the attached bathroom. Then I ran to get her nitro from my backpack. It was in the hallway. Ken and Jude saw me and asked me if I wanted a snack. I said no thank you. I ran back to Grandma and held her spray to her mouth. One spray. She asked me what time it was. After five minutes she'd take the second spray. We waited. She closed her eyes. I held her hand. I sang the song she likes which is "I Wonder as I Wander." And I sang one verse of her favourite CCR song which is "Someday Never Comes." I gave her the second spray. We waited five minutes more. I sang "One Singular Sensation" from *A Chorus Line.* I did the dance from the movie. Then the third spray. If the pain is still there after three sprays we have to call an ambulance. Grandma said the pain was gone. Her forehead was still cold and sweaty. I didn't believe her. I said I was going to call an ambulance. Then she said, No, no, it's not quite time, Swiv. Just hoooooold on, kiddo! It's passing, it's passing. Besides, this is

America! What do you *think*! Okay, shhhhhhhh, I said. Don't talk, don't talk. I put my fingers in her glass of water and threw a few drops onto her forehead. I could hear Ken and Jude clanking around in the kitchen. I sang "Four Strong Winds." I began to cry! Fucking hell! I stopped singing that sad song and sang "Fever" instead. But that reminded me of Mom. I needed her. I tried to sing "You Don't Own Me," Grandma's other favourite song from the 1960s. I turned around so Grandma wouldn't see me crying. I ran to the bathroom and turned on the taps. I ran back to Grandma and sat down on the bed and sang "Fever" in a really, really sexy way so that I would horrify myself into not crying. Grandma started laughing. Don't laugh! I said. Don't talk! Grandma pretended to be disciplined. She clamped her mouth shut and zipped it shut and threw away the key. I felt her forehead. It was normal. I felt her chest. It went up and down. I put my face in the pillow next to hers. Grandma said, Honey, honey. I felt her hand on my head. Then I woke up alone in the bed and it was still the same day which was the longest day ever because of the time change and almost dying four hundred times in water, air and on land. We'd probably almost die in a fire before bedtime.

Grandma and Ken were talking in the living room. Grandma was still wearing Ken's cut-off sweatpants. Jude had gone home to host her book club and to train for Death Valley. She and Ken were going to hike through Death Valley. Ken said he'd be the oldest one there. Aha! said Grandma. You *are* old! When she saw me she said, Welcome to the land of the living! Ken went to the kitchen to get me a snack, which was cheese with blue veins in it and crackers and pieces of mangoes that grew on a tree in Ken's back yard. Does the mango tree cry? I asked Ken. He wasn't sure about that, but good question, he said, he'd listen closely next time. Where's Lou? I asked. I guess he's out walking, said Ken. Or maybe he's at home by now.

Ken and Grandma talked about Willit Braun! Everybody knew Willit Braun. That motherfucker, said Ken. He's still harassing you, huh? Ken said *huh* instead of *eh* because he's an American now. Will he ever stop? said Grandma. They laughed. Such an *officious little dictator,* said Ken. He came to Fresno and accused everybody here of being too enlightened. Too cosmopolitan and too educated and too modern. Ken laughed. Grandma explained to me that when Ken said everybody, that didn't mean everybody in Fresno, just the escaped Russians who had come here from her hometown. She said that sometimes she feels sorry for Willit Braun. He really has not managed to come out from under, has he? she said. Not me, man, said Ken. I don't have a single ounce of pity for that sanctimonious prick. He said that Mooshie — which meant Mom — was such a strong woman. She's a fighter, agreed Grandma.

Why did he say that? Was Mom fighting Willit Braun? She's in a play, I said. Ken asked what play, but Grandma and I couldn't remember the name of it. Then Grandma and Ken talked about how exciting it was that Gord would be born soon. What a trip, man! Won't that be cool having a little . . . said Ken. He held his arms out. We don't know what Gord is, I said. Gord is Gord! said Grandma. Lou is Lou! Let them be! Grandma says that when Mom goes scorched earth. Just let her be!

I am letting them be! I told Grandma. I was just saying we don't know what Gord is! Grandma sang let it be, let it be, let it be, lord let it be. I told her lord wasn't the right word. The right word was *yeah,* let it be, not *lord,* let it be. She's right, said Ken. It's yeah, not lord. Okaaaaaay! said

Grandma. From the top. She sang it again but still used the wrong lyric. She did it on purpose. She just likes opportunities to say lord because it makes her feel like she's praying.

Lou called and said he was home. Ken said he'd drive Grandma over there. Before they left I shoved Grandma's nitro spray into her little red purse and put it right beside the front door, but naturally she forgot it because she was trying so hard to show off all the Beatles songs she knew. She put the word lord into "Don't Let Me Down." Ken didn't tell her lord wasn't in that song. He'd figured out that she just likes putting lord into songs whenever she can.

I stayed at Ken's house by myself for fifteen minutes until he came back. I went into the different rooms and saw pictures of Mom when she was a kid. She looked normal, believe it or not. I saw a picture of Mom holding me when I was a baby. I saw a picture of Lou when he was young with his arm around a beautiful lady. I thought about how Jude was beautiful too. Grandma had told me that all of her six thousand nephews had beautiful wives and girlfriends except for one. He didn't care about all of that, he cared about social justice and rainforests. But then he and his wife got a divorce so I guess he started caring about it after all. I thought about the thong under our bed. I shivered. I looked at Mao. I was as tall as he was in the picture. I went into Ken's bedroom and saw a picture of Jude with her shirt barely on. I screamed. I noticed that my feet had left marks in the carpet in his room. I tried to smooth them out but I made it worse. Finally Ken came home and I tried to keep him from going into his bedroom and seeing his carpet. We played backgammon, Ping-Pong in the garage, speed, super speed, crazy eights, suicide eights, Uno, Skip-Bo and charades. Finally Grandma phoned and said Ken could come and pick her up if he wanted to, but she could also walk, no problem! It was such a beautiful night. Ken had her on speaker phone. I shook my head. She can't walk, I whispered. She's just saying that. She'll definitely die. I sliced my throat with my finger. Ken nodded. He told Grandma he'd be right there. It was so late. No wonder Grandma had watched all those people dying in Fresno. Americans don't really understand that old people like Grandma can't sail around and drink whole bottles of wine in the sun and sing all day and visit with people all night long.

Finally, we were all in bed. Jude had come back to Ken's house after her book club to sleep with him in his bed. She said she loves getting massages from Ken and they use eucalyptus oil! She said Ken has such big, warm, strong hands. Ken looked at his hands. Oh boy! said Grandma. Well, have fun!

Jude said, C'mon, gorgeous. She wanted to go to Ken's bedroom and start getting oil rubbed on her. *Away you kids go!* said Grandma, even though Ken was one hundred years old. I'm glad you're still doing it at your age! said Grandma.

I froze for one second and everything got blurry. I ran into our bedroom and stared at Mao and counted to ten. Grandma came into the room, laughing. Who is that again? she said. MAO! I yelled really loud. Like everything was his fault. I dove into the bed and pulled the blanket over my head. Grandma brushed her teeth in the *adjacent* bathroom and talked to herself about things falling onto the floor but we could find them in the morning — which meant that I would find them in the morning. In the morning I can't bend, said Grandma to herself, and in the afternoon I can't remember! Finally she came to bed. We were lying two feet above Jude's thong. I thought how Willit Braun would not want to be in this house right now. Grandma told me she was so happy that we'd come to Fresno. She moved her head to look hard at me and said, Thank you, Swiv, for coming with me. She was being so serious. You're welcome, I said. It means so much to me, sweetheartchen, she said. I mean it. Thank you. Okay, you're welcome already! I said. I thought about Gord, about how I'd try to be serious with Gord sometimes because it felt a bit nice. For one second. Hoooooo, said Grandma. Are you having regular bowel movements here in Fresno?

Why did she say here in Fresno? Is that another problem with this place? I put my pillow over her face just for one second. She grabbed the pillow and hit me over the head with it. I took it back and put it under my head so she'd stop play-fighting and focus on living. I really needed to see Lou and Ken, she told me. People other than Grandma would have been talking about how they'd almost died from over-drinking and sailing that day, but not Grandma. I think she'd forgotten about all that. I really needed to talk with Lou, she said. What did you talk about? I asked her. We just talked about the truth! said Grandma. Is he suffering? I said. Well, of course, said Grandma.

On and off. Everybody needs to let Lou be Lou. What's his house like? I said. Oh! said Grandma. It's amazing! Every room is filled with things that he's found on his walks. Amazing things. Objets d'art! Beautiful, beautiful antiques and you name it, Lou's got it. He has a hammock strung up on the porch. Does he have a bed? I asked. Somewhere in there, I assume, said Grandma. He has a roommate, too, who is lovely. Is she a beautiful lady? I asked Grandma. In fact, she is! said Grandma. I don't think they're sleeping together, though. Oh my freaking god. Grandma! I'm gonna suffocate you for real! Lou calls her The Presence, like the Dalai Lama, said Grandma. She's an artist and also takes care of the plants at a mall. Lou used to live in the garage after his heart attack but now he's in the house. That's the great thing about California, said Grandma. You can live in a garage year-round!

All your nephews love beautiful ladies, I said. They really do, don't they, said Grandma. Hoooooooo. They really do. Well except for whatshisname, he loved justice and . . . I know! I said. He loved rainforests more, but then changed his mind back to beautiful ladies. Thaaaaaat's right, said Grandma. You remember everything, don't you! She said, "A happiness that forgot nothing, not even murder." That's my friend Albert. What are you talking about, Grandma? I whispered. Rieux sees it in Tarrou's face, said Grandma. Now that is the meaning of life. Right there. Are you drunk, Grandma? I whispered. What? she said. No! I don't think so. Am I? Maybe I am! Joy, said Grandma, is *resistance.* Oh, I said. To what? Then she was off laughing again and there was nothing anybody could do about it.

13.

This morning I got up first to do the assignment that Mom had given me a million years ago and that I'd totally forgotten about, which was to write about Grandma's life. Everybody else, even Grandma, was on California time. She didn't believe in jet lag. Or she was dead. No, she was sleeping. I sat on the floor in our adjacent bathroom with the door shut so Grandma wouldn't be bothered by the light. I put a rolled-up towel on the floor along the skinny line of light that shone through the door. One thing I have to get off my chest is that I found out Ken is a grandpa! He had a wife before Jude. She lives somewhere else. She was also beautiful, according to Grandma — although I'm starting to think that Grandma thinks everyone is beautiful. Ken and his wife had children and now those children have children and live in San Francisco in an *adobe house,* which makes Ken a grandpa who has pictures of naked women in his room and gets massages from them with oil. He loves nudity, just like Grandma. Now I know what people mean about California.

Grandma was born. I'd say when but now I can't remember and she's sleeping so I can't ask her. There were fifteen or seventeen people in the family. Grandma was very curious and roamed around the house like a tiny security guard. When she was two years old she got bored being at home all day and decided to start school. She walked over to the schoolhouse by herself. The teacher let her stay. Her favourite thing to do in school was race for her shoes. All the kids raced for their shoes and tried to get them on first, which was how you won the game. Grandma was too short and fat to keep up with the other kids, who were five years old not two years old, and she didn't even know how to put her shoes on anyway or tie them up. Most of the time she didn't even make it to the pile of shoes because she'd trip or collapse in a heap laughing. She loved that game so much. She still talks about it almost once a month. A lot of the kids in her family started to die and eventually there were only seven left. Now they're all dead except for Grandma. Grandma took me to the graveyard where her six brothers and sisters who were babies when they died are buried in a row that goes from one end of the graveyard to the other. I try to remember all their names when I can't sleep. One of them was Minty. If I have a baby I'll call it Minty even if it's a boy. Minty will be Gord's niece or nephew. Grandma's mom and dad were buried in front of the babies. They have to share a tombstone.

When Grandma was a kid, her friend came over and they accidentally lit the kitchen on fire. Grandma's dad sat in the living room visiting with his brother, and his brother said hey, I think I smell smoke, and Grandma's dad said oh, they'll work it out. Grandma and her friend put the fire out. Afterwards, her dad asked her if she'd learned something. When Grandma was fourteen her dad let her take his car and drive to America to visit her aunt and uncle and bring them a cake. Grandma's mom didn't think it was a good idea but she was always really tired from having babies and from being very sad and up all night praying, so she couldn't do anything about it. Grandma's mom died when Grandma was fifteen years old and it took Grandma forty years to forgive her mom for dying. She didn't know that she was so angry at her mom for dying until she was hypnotized by a friend and found that out. She was also very angry at and fearful of one of her brothers. She felt so much better after finding that out. Then, when Grandma was sixteen, her dad had a stroke and lay in bed paralyzed for nine years until his arm fused onto his chest from never moving it.

Grandma's older sisters were getting married and having children like Lou and Ken. And many, many, many other ones. So her older brothers sent her away to an awful boarding school in the city where she sometimes wouldn't wear the uniform because she didn't feel like it. She was so lonely she thought about throwing herself into the river. One day she stood on the Disraeli Bridge and thought about it. But, right in that moment, a person walked towards her. Was it Willit Braun? I asked her. No, she said, if it had been Willit Braun she would definitely have thrown herself into the river. But that was a half-joke. Grandma jokes all the time and if she's being serious she half-jokes. One day the principal of the school sent her home for not wearing the uniform, and when she got back to the house where she was living with an old lady and another *boarder* the door was locked and she didn't have a key, so she walked in thirty-below weather while her legs were freezing all the way downtown to call her older brother, who came to take her home, at least for the weekend.

After that her brothers sent her to America to be a maid and to go to Bible school. She was so lonely again. And she was so mad at her mom for dying, even though it was irrational to be angry. She couldn't believe how quickly the American's house got messy right after she'd cleaned the whole thing from top to bottom. She started not caring so much about cleaning it. She wished she hadn't cleaned it so well in the beginning because then the American wanted it to be like that every time. After a while she returned home and took her first offer of love, which was from Grandpa, and got married to him. He was young then, like her. He was so skinny that they weighed the same. Grandma had a dream of them becoming circus performers together. She really wanted to wear skimpy little outfits that caught the light and sparkled while she flew through the air on a trapeze or rode on the back of a horse standing up. Or stood on Grandpa's shoulders. But Grandpa wasn't like that. The first time Grandma went driving with Grandpa she noticed how cautious he was and how he followed all the rules. It made her think maybe he wasn't the right guy for her. She really liked to drive fast and break rules. She said that was the only thing that concerned her about Grandpa. Even when she found his lifetime supply of anti-depressants, she wasn't worried, but the way he drove so slowly and cautiously really made her wonder about their future together. Then she decided she had to work at not being bothered by that because she loved him, period.

Grandma's veil caught on fire at her wedding. She was in a hurry to sign her name in the marriage book and get that out of the way but there was a candle beside the book and her veil caught the flame. Her older sister ripped it off her head and stomped on it and then ran home to get her own veil and brought it back to the church and put it on Grandma's head and nobody noticed a thing. The minister said her wedding dress was too wide at the bottom and everyone in the town talked about that for months but Grandma didn't care *one iota.* She ran around at her wedding and wouldn't sit still because she was so excited. Did you play your favourite shoe game at your wedding? I asked her. She said she would have loved to have played it at her wedding. Everyone racing to find their shoes. But Grandpa wanted a more low-key event. Grandpa stood smiling quietly in the reception line while Grandma ran around. He had written all the wedding invitations in his beautiful handwriting. Grandma hated the new *pews* so Grandpa carried all the old wooden pews that she loved out of storage and back into the sanctuary where the wedding was. And they were very heavy. Then he carried them all back into storage after the wedding. She loved Grandpa. She knew she had to do the fighting against everything but that was okay with her. Grandpa didn't like to fight. He liked to read. He made a skating rink for them to skate on together outside in the moonlight behind the little school. They didn't fight with each other. She did the fighting against everything, and that wasn't easy for Grandpa. He thought men should do the fighting and so did the town.

Then Grandma killed her dad. She had to. All of the kids were taking turns waiting around with him to die and the nurses kept having to put a tube down his throat and suck out the liquid that was in his chest so he wouldn't drown in his own body. One night it was Grandma's turn to sit with her dad. She noticed he needed to have the tube. She was already a nurse then, so the other nurses at the hospital said she could just do it herself and not bother them. She decided not to do it because her dad wanted to die and go to heaven to be with his wife. He was calling out to her. He could see her. He told her he was coming to meet her. He said just give him five minutes. Grandma decided to let him go there to meet his wife. She didn't put the tube in. She killed him. And everybody was relieved. After that, it was just life, lots and lots of life. Good times! Fun and games! Grandma learned something about Mom when Mom was two years old, which was just get out of her way and let her do her thing. But Grandpa killed himself later, and then Momo killed herself after that. Grandma just breathed. That was all she could do. For two years she just breathed. She didn't open her mail for a year. She hated people who would talk to her and pretend that Grandpa and Momo hadn't killed themselves. She didn't want to hate people. So after two years she stopped hating people and tried to understand everything instead. She understood that Grandpa and Momo had fought and fought. They were the smartest people Grandma knew. We know that! she said. Mom agreed it was true. Grandma loved Grandpa and Momo. She looks at their pictures a lot. She needed to understand that they had no choice in their minds. They had fought and fought. They had their own fight. They had their own fires. It was their fight. A lot of people in Grandma's town had already died. All her brothers and sisters. There were funerals every day! They kept the coffins open so everyone in town could see the people who had died one last time and say goodbye. But that's life! It's been good! I've been lucky! That's what Grandma says. *Fino alla fine.* My assignment from Mom was complete.

After that, everybody woke up. Grandma sang a song from her favourite band, which is CCR. She was putting lord in the lyrics. Ken and Jude were clanking in the kitchen again. I guess they'd rubbed enough oil on each other for the time being. Maybe they used up all that oil and got cold without their clothes on and figured out that they had to eat or starve to death and be found naked and dead. I imagined Grandma going in there and finding them. It happens! It's life! They're just naked bodies! Relax!

Mom phoned me for one minute today. She asked me how it was going. I said really great if you like being trapped in the Playboy mansion. She said oh hahaha. She said she's so happy for Ken that he's found love. She said she's starting to feel good about the play. It's really coming together. Also, she can see Gord's tiny foot pushing against her stomach from the inside. Will he push right through? I asked. No, no, she said. I've never heard of that happening — like, suddenly a foot? No. I already knew that, obviously, but I was trying to think of things to say so she wouldn't hang up. Mom doesn't understand small talk. Obviously I know that Gord isn't gonna poke his foot right through to the outside of her stomach. She said she missed me and Grandma and isn't spitting oregano oil in the sink. At the end, when we were getting ready to hang up, I said I love you first before she could which I haven't done since I was two years old. And then she sounded so *tragically* excited about it, about me saying it first, that she got all loud and hysterical telling me that she loved me so much too and how really proud she is of me and all that jazz. I said yeah, yeah, yeah well I have to go eat breakfast with sex addicts now. Bye!

Today Grandma and I are going by ourselves to the *old folks' home* to visit all the people Grandma knows who haven't already died. We're taking Ken's convertible! He said Grandma could drive it. She loves driving convertibles in California, she said, which made it sound like she had spent her youth being a movie star and driving around in convertibles every day instead of being a lonely maid in America with a dead mom. She said she'd give me a hundred bucks if I didn't tell Mom she was going to drive Ken's convertible because Mom told her she can't drive anymore. Mom doesn't want Grandma driving around with Gord in the car so she told Grandma in advance that she shouldn't drive anymore so she could get used to the idea. Grandma hated that so much, but Mom said it was just about the natural reaction times of aging people and Gord's life so Grandma had no choice. Mom also said she wanted Grandma to be on the Mediterranean diet and Grandma said it wasn't fair that Mom should torture her in double time with not driving *and* being on the Mediterranean diet. Just to lay those two things on her at once was not on the level, she said. I said I'd stay quiet about the driving for two hundred bucks. Grandma said one hundred and fifty and I said deal because Grandma only lives off Grandpa's pension.

Ken wanted to show Grandma how to drive the convertible but she said she already knew how. Of course I know how to drive stick! she said. What do you *think*? Grandma put it into gear and we lurched into reverse. Lookin' good, man! said Ken. He stood in his driveway and waved good-bye with his big, strong, warm hand.

We drove around and around until Grandma remembered how to get to the old folks' home. She couldn't remember the name of the street or the name of the old folks' home. She just had *feelings* about where it was. All we had to do was drive around and around until her feelings were *made manifest,* she said. The roof was off and Grandma's white hair was blowing straight up from her head. She was wearing her giant welder's glasses and Ken's cut-off UCLA sweatpants. She drove fast. It felt like Grandma was younger now. It felt like I was driving around with Mom or Beyoncé or someone. That's why old people get so furious when young people tell them they can't drive anymore. Aha! Look at that! she said. She had found the home. When she got out of the car she was normal Grandma again, shuffling. I jumped out of the car without opening the door. I hope I don't have to tell you that that's cool. I ran around to her side and slammed on my brakes right beside her and screeched like I was driving a car, too. Ma'am? I said. She took my arm.

We shuffled, shuffled, shuffled. We passed a group of old people standing in a bus shelter right beside the building. A nurse came out and told the old people in the bus shelter, Okay, everybody, we're here! But they hadn't gone anywhere. They walked out of the shelter and followed the nurse back into the building. Grandma told me those were the people who were always trying to escape and go home. The nurses set up a fake bus shelter where they could wait for a bus that never came before going back into the building. That's how they do it now, said Grandma, it's advanced thinking. That's so sad! I said. Well, yes! said Grandma.

The nurse let us in and everyone who was *with it* knew Grandma! Some of them even knew *me*! Grandma had a conversation with her friend Leona. Leona hung on to Grandma's hand and on to my hand really tightly the whole time they were talking so we couldn't escape. Grandma told her about Gord. Babies are wonderful! said Leona. Yes they are, said Grandma. Just wonderful! So wonderful! They were really one hundred percent agreed on that. And I don't mind being ninety because soon I'll get to see Bill! said Leona. Bill was her first boyfriend, who had died before they could get married. Leona was married to someone else for seventy years but she's not as excited about seeing him as she is about seeing Bill because Bill will be seventeen and cute and doing back-flips from a standing position and her ninety-year-old husband will be lying in bed attached to a hose. Grandma and Leona started singing. It was a song about sitting down by the river in Babylon. When they were finished Leona said, Well, we'll soon be dead. That's how it is! said Grandma. That's how it is, said Leona. That was two things they agreed on now. Babies are wonderful and soon they'd be dead. Leona told Grandma to tell Mooshie what a strong girl she is. Tell her! said Leona. I asked Grandma why everyone was saying how strong Mom was. Grandma said because she is and they know it and it's good to be reminded of it. I wondered if I was strong.

We went to have lunch in the dining room with all of Grandma's friends and relatives. She introduced me to them all. Some of them grabbed on to me. Some of them just hung their heads and didn't talk or look at anything. There were bald ladies. Grandma talked to them. She touched their heads and their arms. She spoke to them in their secret language. She kept telling people who she was and then one second later she'd have to tell them again. She kissed them. One of them asked her if she'd heard from Willit Braun lately and then they laughed and laughed. A woman said she just wanted to die already to get away from Willit Braun because she knew she wouldn't meet him in heaven, that's for sure! Even tiny, shrunken, senile people from California with escaping on their minds remembered *the awful reign of Willit Braun.* They sang a lot. An awful lot. Then we ate lunch with them. It was like a nightmare. One woman screamed for help over and over. Help me! Help me! Help me! A man with a hole in his throat that he talked out of asked me if the two of us were getting married! People tried taking off their clothes. Some just sat there and looked dead. Some of them had dolls in their laps. But they all loved it when Grandma sang the old songs with them. I could see she was getting so tired.

It was nap time finally for everyone in the home and we had to go. I thought some of Grandma's friends might not wake up from their naps. The nurses were rounding them up. They were wheeling giant carts of diapers around. The diapers were stacked like books on a bookshelf. One guy had ten stolen yogurts under his shirt and the nurse asked if she could have them back. He tried to fight her. The nurse gave up. Then disaster really struck! Grandma was doing this little dance for two old guys who were her *double cousins,* which means their moms were sisters and their dads were brothers. Grandma said this is the thing that happens in those towns, no problem. The two old guys asked her to do that little dance she did on the porch when she was a kid together with her older sister Irene, who became Lou and Ken's mom. Grandma's old double cousins sang *Pack up your troubles in your old kit bag and smile, smile, smile!* They banged on the plastic arms of their wheelchairs and slid their slippers around on the floor and clapped. Grandma was really entertaining them. They must have really thought they were all kids back on that porch in their old town in the summertime. Grandma twirled around and I could tell she was sort of losing her balance and reaching out to the diaper cart to hold on to, but she missed. I ran over to where she was dancing and then she did a kick that was too high, and then believe it or not Grandma fell down.

Grandma! I ran over to her and kneeled down by her head. There was blood on her face. Nurses came running and lifted Grandma up with the kind of giant sling they use to transfer the whales at SeaWorld and put her on a bed in an empty room where somebody had died two minutes earlier. The dead person's family was still taking out his clothes and slippers from the closet. Grandma looked really confused for a minute but then she started laughing again and saying how she'd be on the DL now. The nurse was saying that her arm looked broken and bruises were forming all over her body. And one of her front teeth was gone. The nurse said if I scrambled around on the floor in the hallway I might find it, but Grandma said oh, for Pete's sake, who needs it? Do you expect the tooth fairy to visit me in the night? She was lisping because of the tooth not being there. That made her laugh harder and then I laughed too and so did the nurses! I didn't want to ask Grandma why she kicked so high during that stupid dance. I didn't want to be mad at her. I tried to think of what Grandma would say instead. What's done is done! Have I learned something? Fun and games! I thought of other things to say. I stood beside her and frowned at her. Grandma started talking to the family of the person who had just died in that room. She knew who they were. They came over to the bed and prayed with her. But you could tell Grandma was in a hurry to get out of there. She said stuff in their secret language like *gownz yenuch fohrdich metten zigh,* which meant they'd prayed enough, God's not dumb, let's get moving.

Grandma started to get up so we could leave but the nurse asked her to lie back down. She wanted Grandma to lie down for one or two hours before we left but Grandma said she didn't have the time for that. The nurses told Grandma she was probably in shock. Grandma told them she thought they might be more shocked than she was. Thank you, Grandma said, but we really have to go. I was carrying Grandma's red purse. Grandma couldn't stop laughing because of the way she sounded, talking without her tooth. I asked Grandma if I should make a splint for her arm. Out of what? said Grandma. She looked around. Let's just skedaddle, Swiv! But it's broken! I said *Jesus Christ* under my breath like Mel Gibson and remembered Mom. I told Grandma if she didn't let me make a splint I'd tell Mom she was driving Ken's convertible. Grandma pretended to be terrified. She put her unbroken hand on her face and made her mouth stretch open like the painting of that guy on the bridge with the bomb behind him. I mean it! I said. Also, I'll tell her that you were dancing and drinking non-stop on the boat. Grandma said she wasn't drinking *non-thtop.* She started to shake from laughing. Okay, I'm leaving, I said. This is your new house. You're staying here forever and wearing diapers. Okay, okay, okay, said Grandma. Thwiv, she said. But then she was laughing *again*! Finally Grandma stopped laughing long enough to ask the nurse if there was a sling she could use, and the nurse went out to find one. When she came back the nurse said she was sorry but she might have to charge Grandma for the sling. She'd try really hard not to. She showed me and Grandma how to put it on over her head and where the Velcro goes and how tight it should be and then Grandma got out of the dead person's bed and we left. On the way out Grandma said goodbye to a thousand people she knew who still hadn't gone for their naps. They were waiting in the hallway. They pointed at her sling and her mouth and she said I know! Isn't it ridiculous! Live and learn! Schpose mitten sigh! Everybody replied, Schpose mitten sigh! They smiled and laughed. Grandma kissed them all again. I made peace signs in lieu of kissing because it was California and also I didn't want them to grab me anymore. I tried to make them not grab Grandma's broken arm when she leaned over to kiss them. Old people love to grab anybody they can get their hands on.

Finally we made it to Ken's convertible. The nurse had tried really, really hard not to charge Grandma for the sling but in the end she gave up and charged Grandma so she wouldn't have to cook the books or lose her job and Grandma told her not to worry one iota about it, she underthtood. The nurse said Grandma would have to get a cast put on her arm. Grandma said hmmmmmm. She wasn't worried. The nurse gave her a T3 for free. Don't tell anyone, she said. She whispered it. Grandma said, What? I said, Don't tell anyone the nurse gave you a free pill. A free pill! Grandma shouted. Well, zut alors! The nurse came to the other side of the checkout desk and hugged Grandma *and* me before I had a chance to escape. She told me to *come back again*! I just nodded and smiled. Please God, let that never happen. I'll give up smoking and swearing. When we were shuffling back to the car Grandma said she had seen *the writing on the wall*. She said hoooooooo. I had her red purse on my shoulder. I felt the nitro spray in the outside pocket. I asked her what she meant. She laughed and said, Oh, just that maybe we should go home a little sooner than we had planned to. We'll surprise Mom! she said. I thought about Grandma all bruised and broken with blood on her face and her tooth missing just suddenly standing there in the living room by the TV for Mom to discover when she came home from rehearsal. Won't that be fun? said Grandma. I tried to change the subject instead of *lashing out,* the way the therapist had told me to do. I knew she would say I was angry with *myself* for not protecting Grandma. But sometimes I was angry at other people, too! I guess the therapist wasn't getting paid enough to deal with the hidden costs of additional anger because Mom did the sliding scale option. Watch this, I said to Grandma. I jumped over the passenger door of the convertible and landed in a perfect sitting position. Ho HO! said Grandma. That's an eleven out of ten. Okay, watch *this*! She pretended to be an Olympic sprinter in a starting block. No, Grandma, no! I yelled. I was lashing out. What the fuck is wrong with you, man! I said. Why can't you just stop doing all these fucking things that are killing you all the time and just fucking be normal! Grandma was quiet then. She stood by the car and moved her good hand on the hood of the car back and forth like she was saying to the car it's okay, it's okay. She said hoooooooooooo. I pulled her nitro spray out of her purse and got out of the car and gave it to her. I had to twist the lid off myself because of her arm. I opened the car door and she heaved herself in there and sat down. We waited five minutes. I didn't sing or dance or talk. We sat in the sun, mad. She didn't use her spray the third time. I'm okay, she said. I'm thorry, Thwiv. I'm sorry too, I said. Grandma looked at her teeth in the rear-view mirror and smiled and moved her face around to different angles like a beautiful model. Not bad! she said.

Then we found out Grandma couldn't drive the car with a broken arm! I'm calling Ken, I said. Hold on, hold on, said Grandma. Just hoooooooold your horses, buckeroo. She made her face go small so she could think. After a minute she told me it was probably time that I learned how to drive stick because she had been six years old when *she* learned and after that had driven to America by herself to deliver a cake and all that. I was trying to be calm and agreeable, instead of lashing out, so I let her teach me. It took a long time to learn. The engine kept stalling. It was really hard. The car was jerking around so much that the radio came on all by itself. Grandma made a joke that we'd be stuck in the parking lot forever just like the old people in the building trying to escape. Somehow that made me learn instantly, and I drove out of the parking lot! I stalled again in the middle of the street. It took four hundred years to move ten feet. The car was jerking so much that suddenly the roof started to come up over us! We couldn't find the right dial to switch off the radio. It was blasting the best of the 80s so loud that even Grandma could hear it and she sang along but not with the right lyrics. Everything was happening at once. The wipers went on. The roof kept going up and down and up and down. We jerked along, singing and yelling. Grandma told me I was doing a great job! We're getting there! But she didn't even really know *how* to get there or where we were going. She didn't care. She just thought it was hilarious that somehow we were moving forward at all.

People in other cars were looking at us like we were escaped tigers or something. I stalled again at a red light. Two teenagers got out of a car beside us and came over to ask if we needed help. They asked Grandma if she'd been in a fight and Grandma said you'd better believe it! They laughed and stood around like nothing serious was happening. Grandma asked one of the boys if he knew how to drive stick and he spread his arms wide like are you kidding me? This is the meaning of my life, driving stick. I was born to drive Canadian children and ancient, bruised ladies around without knowing where to. Grandma said she'd give him twenty bucks to drive us back to Ken's place. I climbed into the little back seat so the teenager could drive. He jumped over the door and landed in a perfect sitting position! Sup! he said. He turned around to fist-bump me. I'm T. I nodded. And you are? he said. S, I said. Awesome! Let's roll. He fist-bumped Grandma on her good hand. He looked at her sling. He said he'd like to see what the other guy looked like and Grandma laughed and laughed like there was no tomorrow. T told his friends to follow us in their car. He turned the radio to a better station and made the roof stay down. I was jealous of Grandma getting to sit beside him. T and Grandma looked like they were in a commercial and had a useless baby in the back seat always getting in the way of their sexy California dates. Grandma didn't know how to tell T how to get to Ken's place. I just feel my way around when I'm in Fresno! she said. I love that! he said. You just feel your way around when you're in Fresno. I love that. He opened the glove compartment and looked at Ken's registration. He found Ken's address. He was careful not to let the glove compartment door bonk Grandma on her knee. He didn't say uncool shit like okay, ladies, don't worry about a thing. I know where to go. Leave it to me. He didn't say anything. He just half-smiled like Lou and made jokes like Grandma. I was dying from how cool he was and how mad I was that Grandma got to sit next to him side by side but life isn't always fair or easy so dot, dot, dot.

T turned off the radio so he could hear Grandma. She told him she wanted to drive past her sister Irene's old house, her sister who was Lou and Ken's mom. Irene once stole silverware from an airplane to give to Grandma as a fancy present when Grandma was a kid and she was the first one in Grandma's family to wear jeans instead of dresses. She thought everything was funny, especially life. T asked Grandma if she remembered the street name. Grandma said maybe Hazelnut, or Nutberry, or Berrynut, or Maplenut or Lingonberry. We were gonna be feeling our way around Fresno for a long time. Want me to call Ken? I said. No! said Grandma. She was *adamantly opposed* to calling Ken, because then she'd have to tell him that her arm had become broken and one of her teeth had been knocked out and a teenager named T was driving us around town. Let me think, said Grandma. Juuuuuuuuuust give me one little minute to think. T and I were quiet in the sun. We had stopped by the side of the road while Grandma made her face small. Then there was a little explosion. I've got it! she said. I remember! Ha! I know *exactly* where to go. T started driving and Grandma said go here, now here, turn right, okay and up there turn right again, now here, now there, now stop!

We were in front of Irene's house. It had been her husband's house too and his name was Benjamin. He'd liked flirting with waitresses and he *really* liked brown eyes. Irene loved him but also he exasperated her seventy-five percent of the time, which meant even when he was sleeping. We all stared at their house. It was an ordinary house. It had a big window in the front and a palm tree in the yard. Grandma stared and stared. T looked at his phone and scrolled and scrolled and scrolled. He had a lot of messages. I looked at my phone. I had one message from Mom trying to use emojis instead of words which she thinks is *fun.*

T probably had a thousand messages from tall California girls in Hollywood asking him to come to their pads to bob around in hot tubs and rub oil on them. Grandma kept staring at her sister's old house. I heard her sniffling. She was crying! In front of T!

I clamped my teeth together and made my lips go small like a butthole and said Jesus Christ. It sounded like *jhzzz kryzzz.* I didn't know what to do to get Grandma to stop crying. If I had a gun I'd just fire an entire *magazine* into the air. T's friends were in the car behind us. They were all looking at their phones and making dates with Rihanna and Taylor Swift and ordering jugs and jugs of eucalyptus oil off Amazon Prime. I looked at my phone too. I fake-texted nobody because the only contact in my phone is Mom. Grandma kept staring at the house. I wondered why you would even want to advertise that your town was the world capital of shrivelled up bits of fruit that everybody hates the taste of. Then T looked at Grandma and said hey, you're sad, that's okay, that's cool! Hey, hey, hey. C'mere. He pulled Grandma's good arm towards him and she flopped against his chest. His chin was on top of her head and he was moving it gently in her white hair. They were hugging! Then T said, Hey S, you too, c'mon dude, group hug! I sort of inched closer to the front seat and then T pulled me closer with one arm and he had his other arm around Grandma and we were all three hugging. It's hard sometimes, said T. Just super fucking hard, right? He patted our backs. I smelled T's chest because my face was smashed against it and I had no choice. What if he was a Bulldog? I liked the way his chest smelled. I felt like I was dying from something. What if Grandma and I were hugging a Bulldog? I wondered how to tell Mom everything that had happened. I decided I wouldn't tell her anything. I'd catch laryngitis on the plane and have it for as long as it took Mom to forget about our trip to California and stop asking questions. Grandma would have to have laryngitis too, but she probably wouldn't cooperate with that. She wouldn't be able to not talk for longer than five seconds. If I had laryngitis and she *didn't* have laryngitis I wouldn't even be able to talk louder than her or change the subject every time our trip came up. Also, how was I going to hide Grandma's broken arm and missing tooth? I would tell Mom just let Grandma be Grandma, the way Grandma talked about Lou. Don't worry about Grandma's bones and teeth! Just let her be! So she fell apart slightly in California, that's her deal, man. Mind your own beeswax! Just go to rehearsal already and forget about it!

Grandma sat back properly in her seat and said hoooooooooo. T moved his chest away from my face and I boomeranged to the back seat really fast so that nobody would think all that hugging had been my idea. Grandma began to laugh. She punched T in the shoulder. Thanks, T! she said. He half-smiled like Lou and said, My pleasure, the pleasure is *all mine.* He started the car again. Grandma looked back at Irene's house. She lifted her arm to wave goodbye and then said oh! It was her broken arm. She laughed. How ridiculous! she said. Then she put her head way back so her whole face was under the sun.

T dropped us off at Ken's place. He knew exactly where to go without feeling his way around. He and Grandma exchanged *contact info.* Grandma doesn't have a cellphone, so he put his name and number and all that into my phone! Now I have two people to get messages from, T and Mom. Even though the messages from T will actually be for Grandma. She invited him and his friends in the other car to come and stay with us any time. T said he'd never been out of Fresno except for once and he hadn't even realized it because he'd been in the trunk of a car but one day, one day! He hugged us again. I smelled his chest really fast, for less than a second. *One last time.*

Ken and Jude couldn't believe that Grandma had broken her arm and lost her tooth at the old folks' home. Oh man, said Ken, that's crazy! No way! Jude wanted to make Grandma lie down quietly but Grandma wanted to be in *the thick of things* not stuffed away by herself in the bedroom with Mao and Jude's thong, so Ken and Jude said she should lie down on the couch and they brought her things like pillows and water and snacks and more painkillers, which believe it or not she dropped all over the floor for me to pick up.

Charge of the Light Brigade! Grandma yelled, right before she swallowed the killers. Ken and Jude just looked at her. Wasn't that a failed mission? said Ken. Grandma was coughing and spilling water and couldn't talk right then. She stared at Ken. She was using her eyes to tell Ken, Of course it was a failed mission! It's just funny! Life is a failed mission! Don't you get it you old hippie grandpa/nephew man? We're all gonna go crazy and die so just have some fun and keep doing it with Jude all over the house! You think all the trees are crying and screaming? You're wrong! They're laughing! Finally Grandma stopped coughing and started telling Ken and Jude about all the people she'd seen at the old folks' home and how we'd had lunch and she'd danced and we'd seen Irene and Benjamin's old house with T. She was huffing and puffing and trying to tell Ken and Jude everything! She told them she'd taught me how to drive stick even though I still didn't really know how. We had a great time! she told Ken and Jude. This is nothing. She pointed at her tooth and arm. It's just pain! It's not life-threatening! That's what I tell De Sica! He'll fix it. They were nodding uh-huh, uh-huh, okay, and smiling and trying to listen, but also trying to figure out what to do about Grandma.

Jude started calling around to hospitals and clinics and insurance people. Should we call Mooshie? said Ken. No! Grandma and I yelled at the same time. You owe me a Coke, said Grandma. You're gonna need a cast, man! said Ken. Grandma looked at her arm. This is the very least of my concerns, she said. She told Ken about the time she fell off a boat into a sea filled with electric jellyfish. Now *that* was an emergency! She started to laugh but ended up coughing again. Jude was getting mad on the phone. She was talking about Grandma's insurance policy. Ken was now also calling people on his cellphone and talking about Grandma and her insurance. Jude and Ken were both pacing around the kitchen talking on their phones. Finally Grandma said never mind! She sat up. She was determined to do something, you could tell. Just never mind with all that! said Grandma. She said hoooooooooo. She put her good hand on her heart. I ran to get her nitro spray from her red purse. She used it three times, which meant we should have called an ambulance but Grandma said no. Ken and Jude talked quietly to each other. We've got to get her to a hospital, said Ken. No! said Grandma. I'm not going. If I get stuck in a hospital here I'll end up with a bill for hundreds of thousand of dollars that I can't pay and I'll never see Gord! They'll never let me get on an airplane. We've got to get to the airport right now, before all this business gets crazy.

Ken called Lou and told him what happened, and Lou rode his bike over to say goodbye to me and Grandma. He had gifts for us: a candle he'd made for Grandma to put in her blue glass candlestick holder from Momo and a small angel for me to hang on my wall. I love you, he told Grandma. You're my heart, man, you're my — Lou cried. I cried and cried then too. I couldn't help it. I wanted to say things like that too. I wanted Lou to come with us. And Ken and Jude. I loved my California cousins. Ken and Jude were still on the phone, trying to change our tickets back to Canada. This is infuriating, man, are they not human beings? said Ken. Stay cool, baby, said Jude. She rubbed Ken's back. I'm trying to tell you! Ken yelled at someone on the phone. Jude looked at me and Grandma like, Oh boy, he's lost his shit! Take cover! But hahaha, as if that fazed us.

Jude gave us snacks for the plane and extra T3s for Grandma that she had left over from an operation on her knee. She has a fake one now. I helped Grandma get back into her track suit. I put her sling on backwards at first. Everything happened and then believe it or not we were driving back to the airport with just Ken, not Lou, because it was too hard for him to keep saying goodbye over and over, man, it was giving him chest pain and he had to go walking for ten or twenty miles to empty his head. He said maybe some day he'd walk to Canada. I really hope he does.

14.

Let's cut to being back home now, because talking about flying with Grandma and her broken arm and petering-out heart, and making connections in Frisco with running and confusion involved and Grandma not taking things seriously and forgetting how many T3s she's taken so she's probably overdosing and laughing about it is almost as exhausting as the trip itself. On the *last leg of the journey* I told Grandma she has a fire inside her and she has to keep it going but she couldn't even talk then and the flight attendant called to have her taken off the airplane on a stretcher.

I ran along beside the stretcher holding on to Grandma's hand and I also had her red purse on my shoulder and my backpack but our little suitcases were with someone else. We were running on the runway. In my head we lifted off and flew and flew, me and Grandma. I held on to her flying bed like it was one of those things Mom gave me when I was a kid to hold on to in the pool and kick like crazy to race her to the deep end.

Grandma loved how fast we were going in the ambulance. There was a mask over her face. She opened her eyes when we took a corner and I fell. She tried to take off her mask with her broken arm but she couldn't because it was in the sling. She tried her other hand, but then the guy in the ambulance said oops, sweetheart, let's leave that where it is for now. She didn't hear him. He went back to typing things into a machine. She pulled off her mask. She said this was the year that Mario Andretti would finally have a shot at the Indy. She tried to point at the driver. The guy said ohhhhkay. He said let's just keep this here for now, okay darling? He put her mask back on. She pulled it off. Are we going to a masquerade party? she said. Grandma, I said. Please, please, please keep it on. She gave me her look pretending to be in big trouble. The guy asked me who I was. Swiv, I said. Great, great, he said, but I mean who are you in relation to . . . he looked at Grandma. Swiv! I said. Are you her granddaughter? Yeah! I said. Grandma loved that. Who else would I be? Like some random kid Grandma had kidnapped to travel around with her? She grabbed me like the old people in Fresno. Her eyes were beaming messages to the guy. Nice, nice, said the guy. He smiled tenderly at Grandma. It's good that you're here, he told me. That's what Grandma had said in Fresno. He asked if I had her list of medications. I got the list out of her little red purse. The guy stared at it. Wow! Is this . . . what do you call it? Cursive, I said. I can't read it either, man. I half-smiled like Lou and T. Grandma squeezed my hand like *I* was the one with problems.

At last we were at the hospital. The guys from the ambulance whooshed Grandma into a room that had curtains for walls, like in our house, and said good luck, Swiv! It was a pleasure meeting you and your Grandma. The nurses took blood from Grandma and knocked her out with some drugs. I told them she had a broken arm and they said they'd X-ray that later and plaster it after getting her levels. Is that new? the nurse asked. She was pointing at the gap from Grandma's missing tooth which everyone could see because her mouth was open while she slept. She was dancing, I said. In California. Ah! said the nurse. She wrote that down. The nurse asked me if I was okay and if I wanted to call someone. She asked me if I had parents or just

Grandma. Grandma's eyes stayed closed. I have all that, I said, yeah. I nodded. The nurse said I should get myself a doughnut and call my parents.

Mom didn't freak out. She was calm. I told her we were home early at the Toronto Western Hospital because Grandma was having a heart attack or something. Mom said okay, honey, listen. I'll be there in fifteen minutes. Why don't you go get yourself a doughnut or something. I hung up and wandered down a hallway. I went into a washroom that was huge but only had one toilet in it and bars to hang on to. I sat on the toilet without *using* the toilet and hung on to the bars. Where the holy hell was I supposed to find a doughnut and what good would it do? I hung on to the bars by the toilet and sat there and sat there. My head kept flopping over and back up again. I couldn't control it, like Grandma. Then Mom and a different person with four thousand keys on a ring were standing in the washroom. The person said, Here she is, Mama! Oh my god, said Mom. She bolted towards me. Oh my god, they didn't know where you were. I went to get a fucking doughnut! I said. I had fallen asleep sitting on the toilet. I jumped up. I didn't want to be found passed out on a toilet like a depressed celebrity. Mom tackled me and pinned me against the wall and hugged me forever while the person with the key said, Okay, I'll leave you two here for a bit but this is a handicapped washroom so you'll have to vacate it sooner or later, my friends. Gord was crushed in between me and Mom. We were so happy to be together. I was so happy that Mom was there. I'm serious about that. It was a true feeling. California had changed me, man.

Mom and I jogged down the hallway to Grandma. Mom held her giant stomach up with one hand. I held her other hand. We were all connected to each other like a search party. Grandma was awake and talking to the nurse when we got to her room. She was talking about California. Oh! she said. Entrez! Entrez! Bienvenue! They told me you'd gone for a doughnut! Then we had to tell Mom the whole story of California, except for the part about Grandma driving. Mom and I sat on each side of Grandma. Mom was on Grandma's good side so she could hold her hand, and I put my hand on Grandma's soft stomach. I tried to keep my hand loose so it could bounce. I watched it bounce up and down on her stomach when she laughed. Mom tried to say things that were serious but Grandma only wanted to talk about things she thought were hilarious, like when I lost control of her wheelchair and she went flying off and plowed into the Body Shop stand, or things she thought were beautiful, like when Lou held her close in the boat so she wouldn't fall overboard. And then she went back to talking about hilarious things like when she fell at the old folks' home from kicking too high. I poked Mom to make her smile.

Telling this story made Grandma laugh so hard that the nurse from way over at the *nurses' station* came to tell us we were in a hospital. What did she say? said Grandma. She said we're in a hospital, I told Grandma. What the blazes? said Grandma. She said we're in a hospital! I shouted at Grandma. Boy, I'd love a cup of coffee, said Grandma. Small black. Grandma talked, and I looked at Mom looking at Grandma. I watched her for a long time. You're strong, I said. Mom turned to look at me. That's what everyone in California said. Really, Swiv? said Mom. She didn't know what to say. I thought she was going to start crying and have to blow her nose forever. Really? she said again. I nodded. Her face turned red. She tried to hide how happy she was about being strong by making a dumb face. But I knew she was strong and happy. My hand bounced off

Grandma's stomach ten times in one minute and I put it back gently every time. If your Grandma is laughing so hard that your hand which is on her stomach bounces off ten times in one minute how many times will it bounce off her stomach in one year? Five million, two hundred and fifty-six thousand times.

Then Mom was telling us about her play. I could see she thought the director was an asshole. She mostly just hates directors. But she likes her understudy a lot. So your stage manager isn't mad at you anymore? I asked. No, I think she is again, said Mom. She had stopped being mad at me but now she is again.

Some nurses came into Grandma's room and fiddled around with things. They didn't talk loudly enough to Grandma so Mom and I always had to repeat everything they said. Did she say they were bringing me a sandwich and a cup of coffee? asked Grandma. They're waiting for a bed in cardiology! I said. Grandma wasn't supposed to eat or drink but she kept offering me a hundred bucks to go get her a black coffee. The nurses put another oxygen mask on Grandma's face to get her to stop talking. Just kidding. But she stopped talking. She closed her eyes. Mom was doing the crossword puzzle. Who wrote *The Grapes of Wrath* again? she said. How the blazes should I know! I said. Google it! Mom said no, her rule for crosswords was no googling. Why can't I remember the guy's name? she said. This is nuts! All your brains have gone to Gord, I said. It's true! she said. Did all your brains go to me when I was in there? I asked her. Of course they did, she said. Oh, but then you grew another brain to give to Gord? I asked. That is *exactly* what I did, sweetheart! she said. So I have your old brain and Gord has your new brain and you have no brain, I said. Until you grow another one. John Steinbeck! she yelled. Grandma's eyes pinged wide open. She pulled off her oxygen mask and smiled. I'm still here! she said. Did you have dreams? I said. Yeah! said Grandma. Of somebody getting me a black coffee! She wanted to talk about John Steinbeck. Would you saw up *The Grapes of Wrath*? I asked Grandma. She said oh yeah, she'd saw up any book if it was too big.

Grandma told us about her favourite scene from *all of literature,* which was in *The Grapes of Wrath.* It's where a girl who is pregnant and travelling to California with her poor family and some other people *loses* the baby, and then even though she is sad and starving and scared she feeds an old man, who is also sad and starving and scared, milk from her own *breasts* so he won't die. Grandma read that book long ago in secret because everything was banned in her town. Mom and I looked at Grandma. I mean that is it, in my opinion, she said. That's what? said Mom. But Grandma had fallen asleep again. I asked Mom if she would let an old man drink from her body if she lost Gord. She didn't answer for a long time. She sighed. If he was starving to death? she said. I nodded. Right there next to you in a barn, I said. Would you let a person drink from your body when you're suffering and just trying to get to California? Mom sighed again. Swiv, she said. I want to say yes. I really want to say yes. I waited. I thought to myself. Then say yes already! She made her face small to think, just like Grandma. I had never seen Mom thinking so hard before. I would *hope* that I would, she said. That's what I can answer truthfully right now. Is that your final answer? I said. Then the nurse came in and said, Oh, oh this isn't . . . she stared at the machine by Grandma's head. She started fiddling around with it again and then she pushed the intercom button on the wall. Mom stood up. What?

she said. Is there a problem?

What's happening? I said. I had Lou's angel in my backpack. I snuck it onto Grandma's stomach under the hospital blanket while Mom and the nurse were busy staring at the machine. I moved Grandma's hand on top of the angel so she could feel it.

The nurses brought Grandma to intensive care. They stuck a hose down her throat that did her breathing for her so she could just rest. It was taped to her cheek. The corner of her mouth was stretched out from the hose. There was blood in the corner of her mouth. It was so noisy. It was as loud as the arcade at Dufferin Mall. Machines were beeping and blowing air and dinging and gurgling. They wanted to pack Grandma in ice. They asked Mom if she would try to slide Grandma's wedding ring off her finger. Mom tried to get it off but couldn't get it over Grandma's giant knuckle. Grandma didn't even know Mom was trying to steal her jewellery. You should try eucalyptus oil, I told Mom. She didn't hear me. There were nurses clustered around Grandma. Mom kept having to move out of the way. Gord kept knocking against Grandma's hose. The nurses told me and Mom to sit in a little room down the hall for a few minutes. One of them patted Mom's stomach. They'd come and tell us when to come back.

Mom and I went into the little room, and then believe it or not Mom wet her pants. She must have worried that she hadn't prepared me for reality by embarrassing me enough times so would just try to fix that right away. What the holy hell! I said. Mom! Oh my God, said Mom. It's my fucking water. *Zhhhhzhus Khrssst.* She said Jesus Christ the way I'd said it in California. It was cool and funny how she said it with her teeth clenched and her mouth all puckered. I had inherited cool things from her after all.

15.

This next part is for Grandma who likes speed and laughing. She likes stories to be fast and troublesome and funny, and life too. She doesn't like hauling epic things around. Which is why she saws up her books. I forgot to tell you that Grandma is part Christian and part *secular existentialist.* Mom told me that. I just found that out when I filled out the religion part of Grandma's hospital form. Will she want to see a chaplain? A rabbi? A priest? I read these out to Mom. Mom said Grandma wants to see Gord. I wrote down *Gord.*

Mom and I were standing in four feet of *broken water* in the little room next to where Grandma was hooked up to the hose and getting packed in ice. Two nurses came and took Mom to a different part of the hospital in a wheelchair. I ran along beside them. I did a cartwheel for Mom. One of the nurses said to the other nurse, That's just what girls her age do non-stop. She said my legs were totally straight in the air. I did another two cartwheels for Mom and the nurse before we deked into an elevator. Mom smiled, but like she had sort of forgotten how. Then Mom was being *examined.* I was sitting alone in another room with a TV hanging from the ceiling. How the blazes was I supposed to turn it on way up there? I coughed from nervousness. The nurse came back and told me Mom was eight inches dilated. That was a horrific mental picture, but I nodded and smiled. I wanted to say Mom's and my signature *Zhhhhhzhus Khrssst* but the nurse was all business, man. Do you know what that means? the nurse said. I nodded again. It means she's in labour, said the nurse. Duh, no kidding, lady! I *wanted* to say. But I smiled and nodded again for the forty-ninth time. The nurse came over and put her hand on my arm. Do you speak? she said. I nodded fast, the way Grandma's head does when it involuntarily shakes. I tried to let sound out of my mouth. Your mom's gonna be fine, said the nurse. She rubbed my arm. Do you — is your — is there another adult we could call to be with you?

Dot. Dot. Dot. Well??? Someday never comes! You have to figure that out fast, when you're a kid. That's the CCR song that Grandma loves. I play it for her in the morning to get her blood moving. ENNA-way.

The nurse gave up on me saying anything just as some words finally came out. *It's too soon.* The nurse put her hand on my arm again like it was the talking stick from group therapy and she didn't have permission to talk without holding on to it. No, honey, she said. It's fine. It's a bit early but every-thing is fine. I knew she was going to sug-gest that I go and get a doughnut. Why don't you go get a snack? she said. I said, Mmmmm. I didn't want her to go. I was waiting for her to say doughnut. Like what kind? I said. Oh, just whatever you want. Do you have money? I said, Mmmmm. How much do I need? She said that depends on what I'm getting. For instance? I said. The nurse said, For instance a chocolate bar or a granola bar is about two bucks I think, from the vending machine. A bag of chips might be less. Hmmmm, I said. And if I went to the Tim Hortons in the main lobby? Oh, well, there, yeah, you could get a snack there, that's true. Hmmmm, I said. Like . . . ? The nurse said I could get myself some Timbits or a muffin. I nodded. Or . . . ? I said. You could get chocolate milk or a scone, she said. This was fun. It was like being with Grandma. She knew I wanted her to say doughnut! You could even get a . . . she said. I smiled. Here it comes! I thought. You could even get a bagel with cream cheese! she said. I loved this nurse. I started laughing, sort of. I slumped my shoulders. The nurse laughed. Or a doughnut! she said. I stopped slumping and jumped up as high as I could and punched the air. Yessssss! I said.

I went to the Tim Hortons in the lobby and came back with three doughnuts and stared at the TV I couldn't reach and wasn't even turned on. What a waste of taxpayers' money. The nurse came back out. She said Mom was coming along nicely. I could go in and see her. When I went in, Mom was on her hands and knees on the floor and grunting and moaning. That didn't seem to me like *coming along nicely.* I went over and put my hand on her back. She said, Swiv, Swiv, I'm fine, I'm fine, don't worry. Do you want a doughnut? I asked her. She said not right then. She made a horrible sound, like a wild animal. She was turning into a werewolf. She lifted one of her arms and pawed at my throat. Um, okay, Mom, I said. Don't forget about what I said. You're strong. I whispered it into her werewolf ear.

Gord would be too terrified of Mom now to come out. Maybe Gord would be a werewolf too. I'd have to raise a werewolf by myself. I stood next to Mom but from a safe distance. I didn't know what to do or say. I looked around and smiled at the nurse. I wanted to tell her that I was a normal person even though my Mom was on her hands and knees growling.

The nurse left the room and I leaned over to whisper to Mom. I asked her why she was rehearsing for a play that she couldn't even be in now because she was having Gord. Did you get your wires crossed? I asked her. She stopped grunting and snarling. The contraction was over and for two seconds she switched to being a human being again. Oh, I'll explain that later, she said. She started moaning again and said I should go see how Grandma was doing and then come back. What a relief that was. I sprang away from her. I told her I'd be back in a second but secretly I planned to stretch that out into three minutes. Three minutes of werewolf time.

I ran to see Grandma. I got lost four hundred times in all the hallways and steel doors and forgot what floor she was on. Finally I found the signs to the ICU and followed them. The door to the ICU was locked and they had to buzz me in. It was really noisy and hectic inside, with nurses stomping and gliding around and looking serious in their blue and green uniforms with vee necks and big pockets and blue gauzy shower caps. There was Grandma! She wasn't packed in ice anymore. Now she was almost naked. She sure will love to tell this story, I thought. Too bad there wasn't a soldier or some other man around she could show her body off to. The nurses swarmed around her. Her eyes were sort of open. She couldn't talk because of the hose. I ran over to her and said Mom was having Gord right now! Grandma's eyes got bigger. Now they were really open. The nurses said, Wow! Here? Yeah, I said. Upstairs! Or downstairs. I wasn't sure. Grandma started pulling at the hose and trying to sit up. She was going to run naked out of the ICU to see Gord! Whoops, Elvira, said the nurse. They knew her name! We need you to lie still a tiny bit longer, sweetie. Grandma shook her head and tried to sit up again. Her eyes told me to come close to her ear and tell her everything that was happening. Mom's having Gord, I said. She's nearby, upstairs or downstairs, in a room. She's kneeling. There are nurses there, too. Everything's fine. I didn't tell Grandma that Mom had turned into a werewolf. Grandma kept nodding and making her eyes go big at me to keep me saying things. I got some doughnuts, I said. Grandma nodded. Mom's water broke all over the floor. Grandma blinked her eyes at me. Seriously, I said. We almost drowned. I thought it was too early for Gord to be born but the nurse said it wasn't and Mom said she'd talk about that later. This is the sound she makes. I made the sound of a werewolf, but not as terrifying as the actual sound Mom made. Grandma was laughing with her eyes. She was blinking. Tears were coming out of them.

Okay, said a nurse. She was looking at Grandma's machines and tapping her pen. We should let her rest a bit more now. This nurse told the other nurses that the levels had changed. She read out numbers that the other nurse wrote down. One nurse stood there with her hand on Grandma's shoulder, the one without the sling, to keep her from taking off to see Gord. I told Grandma that I had promised Mom I'd be right back. She nodded. Then I told Grandma that I'd come back to her after that. I kissed her forehead. I thought about how Grandma had given Mom her brain a million years ago when Mom was inside her and now Gord and I had Mom's brains.

How long would it take for Mom to grow a new one? Grandma closed her eyes like she was so happy and like she was kissing me back. I'll be back in a sec! I said. In two shakes of a lamb's tail! Grandma raised her good thumb. Bye, Swiv, said the nurses. Can't wait to meet Gord! Somehow Grandma had told them everything.

I whipped back to Mom and Gord. Mom was in a bed properly now, except for waving her rosy parker around for everyone in the universe to feast their eyes on. Her legs were up in the air and she was still growling. Someone was pulling Gord out of her. Stand here, stand here, said a nurse. You really shouldn't be here. Mom said, Stay! The nurse put a gown on me and tied a mask around my face. I stood by Mom's leg. I didn't know what to do. I put my hand on her knee. It was quivering. The nurse told Mom to breathe. Yeah, Mom! I said. You heard the lady! Breathe! Mom growled instead like she was planning to kill all of us as soon as she got Gord out of there. Breathing is the main thing in hospitals. That's all they want you to do whether you're young or old and even if it's with a hose. Breathing and eating doughnuts. Mom was still growling. It was like she had two thoughts in her head. Have a baby. Kill people. I wondered if I should warn the nurses that they were dealing with a very difficult lady. But then, believe it or not, Gord slithered right out of Mom's butt and voila!

P.S. I know it's not her butt, okay? Don't ever talk to me about those things.

A lot of things happened then. Just watch *Call the Midwife* if you have a TV and you'll know what I mean. The nurses plunked Gord on top of Mom, which made her cry. I heard her thinking, Oh, fuck, *this* is Gord? But that wasn't why she was crying. They were *tears of happiness,* which is the first time I've heard of this. But that's Mom. She's missing a brain now. She's getting her emotions backwards. She grabbed me. I was face to face with Gord who was covered in blood and guts. Mom gripped us like we were the last two golden tickets in *Charlie and the Chocolate Factory.* Nothing could stop Mom from squeezing us to death. Maybe with all that growling and crawling around she had become the kind of wild animal that kills its babies out of jealousy because they're young and good-looking. My oxygen levels were low like Grandma's. Breathe, Gord! Breathe! I said in my head while I was suffocating to death. King of the Castle is such a stupid thing, was my last thought.

But as you probably guessed by now, we lived. Mom said I should check on Grandma. She tried to put herself into Gord's mouth. Gord screamed because who wouldn't scream if suddenly someone was jamming a part of their body into you. Mom forced me into the bed with her and Gord. She wanted all three of us to lie there and take a selfie for Grandma. Gord was so short. It was hard to get us all in the frame. Okay, Flopsy, I said to Gord. Say cheese. I kissed Gord's greasy head and Mom's sweaty cheek. I slithered quietly off the bed. I had to go see how Grandma was.

I ran to the ICU and waited for an authorized person to go through the locked door so I could sneak in behind them. Grandma was there in her bed. Only two nurses were fiddling around her now. I looked at her chest. The young nurse saw me. Has Gord arrived? she said. Yes! I said. I shouted it. Grandma didn't open her eyes. Congratulations! said the nurse. Grandma still didn't open her eyes. The machines were so loud. Where was the angel from Lou? The nurse told me that Dr. De Sica had come to see Grandma, that he'd heard she was in the ICU. I smiled and nodded. Grandma would have been so happy to see him. Was she awake? I asked. No, unfortunately, said the nurse, she was sleeping. He left a note for her. The nurse asked me if I wanted to give Grandma an ice chip. She told me to hold it on Grandma's tongue and let it melt there. The hose was still in her mouth. It was taped to her cheek. Her lips were chapped and there was still dried blood on the corner of her mouth because the hose was tearing it a bit. I held the ice chip on her tongue. Her tongue didn't move even when I put the cold ice chip on it. In my head I heard her say *Na oba*! in her secret language. I said, Grandma, Gord is here. I put my phone with the photos right by her eyes. I scrolled so she could see all of them. But she didn't open her eyes. The young nurse said, Honey, let's let Grandma rest now. She said they were doing a shift change and I could come in the morning. She said it was late and wow, what a busy day, eh? I should sleep. I took a photo of Grandma for Mom and Gord.

I ran back to Mom and Gord, but they weren't where I'd left them. They'd been moved to some other room that had a window. They were sleeping together in the bed even though Gord had a little plastic box to sleep in next to Mom. Gord was wearing a toque. I leaned over the bed with the picture of Grandma, but they didn't open their eyes. Everybody was asleep and I didn't know what to do. I sat in a chair beside Mom and Gord. Mom had told me I should use her phone to call people about Gord and Grandma. But where was her phone now? I wanted to call Lou and Ken. Gord's here, man! Crazy, right? I remembered I had T's *contact info* in my phone for Grandma. I texted him some pictures of me and Mom and Grandma and Gord. In between all his messages from the sexy hot tub girls in Hollywood he'd have a picture of Grandma connected to a hose. And a random Canadian family missing certain members.

Then I remembered something from *Call the Midwife.* I emptied everything that was in my backpack onto the chair. I took my jean jacket off and lined my backpack with it so it was soft and warm in there. I carefully, carefully, carefully put Gord into my backpack. Mom didn't move or make a sound. Some parent! She was obviously lying to me when she said new mothers never sleep. Gord's toque was poking out of the top of my backpack. I took it off and put it in my pocket and pulled the strings on my backpack a bit so there was still an air hole for Gord. I put my backpack on my front. Gord was heavier than I'd thought. Whoa! Props to Mom for hauling Gord around like this everywhere. Now I knew why she was so exhausted all the time. I took a big sheet off the shelf and put it over my backpack. I tied it around my neck. It drooped down to the floor. I looked like the pope. I heard a squeak. I jiggled my backpack a bit under the sheet. Me and Gord took off to the ICU. The lights in all the hallways were dim. There was hardly anybody around, just janitors and tired-looking people who were waiting for something or someone. Me and Gord waited for an authorized person to go through the ICU door. I stayed a long distance behind the person and pretended to be reading a sign on the wall about diarrhea and vomiting. But the authorized person didn't go in! He was standing there talking with someone. Gord squeaked again. I ran into a different little room for bereaved people and whipped off the sheet. I stuck my finger into the top of my backpack and felt around for Gord's mouth. I kept my hand there. It felt like Gord would suck my finger right off and choke on it. I could hear Mom yelling at me for killing Gord with my finger and not even caring that I was as a result *missing* a finger. I couldn't get the sheet back over us. I ran back out and believe it or not was just in time to sneak in through the open ICU door.

We ran over to Grandma. There were no nurses standing around her this time. They were at their station writing things down. They didn't see us. Grandma's eyes were closed. The tube was gone. I pulled Gord out of the backpack. Grandma! I said. I gently put Gord down on Grandma's bosom. Grandma! I said. This is Gord! Grandma opened her eyes. Gord! she said with her eyes. You have *got* to be kidding me! What *a sight for sore eyes*! Welcome to the land of the living! She slowly put her hand on Gord's hairy back. Gord nestled in there. Grandma tried to grab me and this time I let her. Grandma! I said. Wake the blazes up! Gord is here! I was shouting right into her ear. Gord woke up and started squeaking. It sounded like, What the holy hell is happening, man. Gord's head swivelled around. Grandma smiled. I couldn't get out of her grip. She was trying to move her head down to get a closer look at Gord. She was trying to say something. Nothing came out. I held Gord up right in front of Grandma's face. Grandma! I said. I've got a sister! I've got a sister!

Then there was an explosion by the

nurses' station. It was Mom. She had some-how got in through the ICU door — prob-ably by slitting somebody's throat — and she was yelling at the nurses to tell her where her mother-fucking family was. Scorched earth, man. Unleash the hounds. After seeing her growling and crawling around on the floor and exposing her wazoo *all over tarnation* and shoving her knockers into people's mouths *like there was no tomor-row* there was nothing that could embarrass me anymore. I waved at Mom all casual, like oh hey, hi, we're just here by the pool having chocolatinis. I was trying to calm her down. I tried to say something but Grandma was suffocating me with her broken arm. I picked up Gord and held her in the air to show to Mom. Over here! I squeaked. I tried to make it sound like a baby saying it so Mom would laugh. Over here! Over here!

What the fuck! said Mom when she saw me waving Gord around. She's not a pup-pet, Swiv! I mistakenly thought Mom would be in a good mood after having located her goddamn newborn! She shuffled over to us, all hunched over and fuming. She was hold-ing her stomach. There were two gigantic wet splotches on the front of her hospital gown. They were growing right before my very eyes! Grandma made a sound. Was she laughing? Mom took Gord and began to sway. She calmed down. She went closer to Grandma. My jean jacket fell off Gord and she was naked. Mom hadn't even had the *common decency* to put a diaper on her. Gord had some kind of tubing sticking out of the place where her belly button should have been. Grandma didn't even notice. Her eyes were closed. Mom! I said. I pointed at Gord's stomach. Oh, that'll fall off, don't worry, said Mom. I picked up my jean jacket and wrapped it around Gord again. Parts of her body are falling off. Turns out people have issues right from the very get-go. Gord's face was red and splotchy like she'd been screaming for help inside Mom for the last nine months. Her hair was greasy but it was sticking out really well. I liked it. I'd never comb out her tangles. I would help her escape from Mom if Mom tried to comb them out. We all squeezed in next to Grandma on her skinny bed. Mom was holding on to all of us. Gord was pinned under Mom's arm and I was pinned under Grandma's arm except she didn't know it.

Mom, said Mom. She was whispering into Grandma's ear. We're going to name Gord after you. You're gonna name Gord Grandma? I said. I was whispering. I thought Gord was Gord. Some nurses came running over then. Just let us be us! I heard Grandma yelling in my head. The young nurse showed us a little note that Grandma had written when she was still attached to the hose. She gave it to Mom. Mom read it to me and Gord. *My friends, I'd like to negotiate my surrender!* What does that mean! I said.

Gord lay there with us making small noises and small movements. I let her hang on to my finger. The nurse said Grandma had asked them to take out the hose. So she could talk? I asked. So she could die, said Mom. Mom was crying but she was smiling *and* crying because Mom is Mom. *All over the map!* I put my hand on Grandma's stomach. Maybe she would laugh now. Shake, I said in my head. Please shake. Mom told Grandma we were going to be okay. I waited. Mom told Grandma she could go. C'mon, shake! Mom told Grandma we loved her so much, that Momo and Grandpa and Irene and her mom and dad and all her four thousand dead brothers and sisters were waiting for her. Mom kept making lists of people for Grandma. Seems like there were four hundred billion people waiting around somewhere for Grandma to get the party started. Then Mom was singing Grandma's favourite

CCR song. Tears were falling onto my arm from Mom, who was still trying to smile while she cried. Gord made little squeaks in my jean jacket. Mom was singing "Someday Never Comes." Then we both sang Grandma's other favourite song. *For poor on'ry people like you and like I . . . I wonder as I wander out under the sky.*

I waited for Grandma's stomach to shake. It didn't shake. She'd grab me soon and say, Aha, gotcha! The nurses quietly went away. Grandma, Grandma, I said. I'll give you a hundred bucks. Grandma! I said. Fight!

16.

Here's a question for you, Dad. If three people go into a hospital and one of them dies, how many people will leave the hospital? If you're our family, it's still three. That's the problem with our family. Or it's the problem with problems. I'm not gonna sit around outside throwing clothespins into the bucket to make Grandma come back. *Just put me in a pickle jar and run outside and play.*

I have videos of Grandma on my cellphone. In one I asked her what will happen to her body after she dies. She says ahhhhh, my body! My body will become energy that will light your path. I can hear her yelling at the Raptors. Stay in it! Box out! Arms up! And I can hear her talking about those sharks that survive by playing dead. And about bioluminescence. And about Mom. And about you. And about fires inside us. And about fighting. And about Grandpa and Momo. And what fighting is, even when it's making peace. Hooooooooooo. You never win games in the exact same way, always adjusting, changing, thinking. Defence is always key. You have to guard. Hoooooooo. Mom and Gord and I are still in the same house. It's a bit of a disaster. I wrote to T pretending to be Grandma. I said *greetings and salutations T! How goes the battle?* He texted back and said *WTF. Who this. ID or b block.* I don't know what to text next but I think that's how love goes.

Lou is walking to Canada! I asked Mom if she'd want to bang Lou or at least be his girlfriend. She's beautiful enough, I think, almost, to be his girlfriend. Mom said no. She said, Ew, Swiv, no. We're cousins! That's not normal. So believe it or not, now Mom has finally decided to take an interest in being normal. Better late than never! I asked Mom what *on'ry* means. You mean like in the song? she said. *Poor on'ry people like you and like I?* She said she thought it meant all riled up. As in ornery, she said. Are we poor, ornery people? I asked her. She told me that from now on she was going to write her own plays and direct them. She says she just does not jive with directors even though the word is jibe. She's still doing the play. I'm going to take care of Gord backstage so Mom can come flying back there and feed her between scenes. Gord is hilarious most of the time. And the rest of the time she's a basket case. She really takes after Mom.

I read Grandma's letter to Gord the other day. *You're a small thing and you must learn to fight.* And today I saw one tiny blue pill on the floor under the table where Grandma sits. Bombs away, Swiv! I heard her say. Man, you should have seen how fast I fell to my knees.

ACKNOWLEDGEMENTS

I'm deeply grateful to Sarah Chalfant and Lynn Henry. And also to Erik! Underlined three times. And, finally, to my revolutionary mother, Elvira Toews, for teaching me, ceaselessly, when to fight and how to love.

Brief lines from the following works are gratefully quoted: on page 18, from "And Death Shall Have no Dominion," a poem by Dylan Thomas; on page 40, from *The Designated Mourner,* a play by Wallace Shawn; on page 83, from *Guest of Reality,* a novel by Par Lagerkvist; on pages 89–90, the line "what makes a tragedy bearable and unbearable is the same thing — which is that life goes on" is a variation on a sentence from "Hiding in Plain Sight: Natalia Ginzburg's Masterpiece," an article by Cynthia Zara in the *New Yorker,* June 22, 2017; and on page 250, from *The Plague,* a novel by Albert Camus.

ABOUT THE AUTHOR

Miriam Toews is the author of seven previous, bestselling novels: *Women Talking, All My Puny Sorrows, The Flying Troutmans, Irma Voth, A Complicated Kindness, A Boy of Good Breeding,* and *Summer of My Amazing Luck,* and one work of non-fiction, *Swing Low: A Life.* Her books have been widely published internationally, and adapted for stage and film. Among other honours, she is the winner of the Governor General's Literary Award for Fiction, the Libris Award for Fiction Book of the Year, the Writers' Trust Fiction Prize, and the Writers' Trust Marian Engel/Timothy Findley Award. She lives in Toronto.

The employees of Thorndike Press hope you have enjoyed this Large Print book. All our Thorndike, Wheeler, and Kennebec Large Print titles are designed for easy reading, and all our books are made to last. Other Thorndike Press Large Print books are available at your library, through selected bookstores, or directly from us.

For information about titles, please call:
(800) 223-1244

or visit our website at:
gale.com/thorndike

To share your comments, please write:
Publisher
Thorndike Press
10 Water St., Suite 310
Waterville, ME 04901